Agents of the Internet Apocalypse

Also by Wayne Gladstone

Notes from the Internet Apocalypse

Agents of the Internet Apocalypse

Wayne Gladstone

Thomas Dunne Books
St. Martin's Press
New York

This is a work of fiction. All of the characters, organizations, and events portrayed in this novel are either products of the author's imagination or are used fictitiously.

THOMAS DUNNE BOOKS.
An imprint of St. Martin's Press.

www.thomasdunnebooks.com
www.stmartins.com

Designed by Steven Seighman

Library of Congress Cataloging-in-Publication Data

Gladstone, Wayne.
   Agents of the internet apocalypse : a novel / Wayne Gladstone. — First edition.
       p. cm.
   ISBN 978-1-250-04839-4 (hardcover)
   ISBN 978-1-4668-4925-9 (e-book)
 1. Internet—Fiction.   I. Title.
   PS3607.L3436A73 2015
   813'.6—dc23

                                        2015015542

St. Martin's Press books may be purchased for educational, business, or promotional use. For information on bulk purchases, please contact the Macmillan Corporate and Premium Sales Department at 1-800-221-7945, extension 5442, or write to specialmarkets@macmillan.com.

First Edition: July 2015

10 9 8 7 6 5 4 3 2 1

For the three magical weirdos: Asher, Sage, and Quinn

Part I

1.

There are certain fibers in the world. Man-made. Artificial. And sometimes, we take those fibers and weave them through something natural. Rayon stitched into cotton with systemic efficiency, creating enough support to form things like a hospital blanket. The label says cotton, but if you wrap it around yourself at 3 A.M., letting it rub up against your cheek in a failed attempt at comfort, you'll only feel what's fake, like trying to absorb the warmth of a baby chick through a wire fence.

The blanket doesn't soften with time. You can't wear it smooth like a waterfall over rocks; crags turning to silk over centuries. Your efforts only destroy the good parts. Nature fails, the cotton wanes, and the man-made network of interlocking fibers holds only itself together, providing neither warmth nor comfort, despite technically still being a blanket.

"You're writing about the Internet again," Dr. Kreigs-man said, closing my journal and placing it on my hospital bed.

Unlike my first therapist, Dr. Kreigsman had read my journal, thinking it provided valuable insight. Dr. Laurent, however, had said such efforts weren't necessary. Of course, she seemed to believe a psychiatrist's duties were limited to prescribing pills and asking about sexual side effects. She was also good at never debating. At any prickly point in our talk therapy, she'd go limp, frown slightly, and say, "I won't argue with you" as if the desire for answers was, itself, a sign of mental illness.

The third time she tried that, I held the fingertips of my left hand to my chest like a sane gentleman and said, "I'm sorry, Dr. Laurent, let's get back to the important discussion of maintaining erections while medicated."

"Now you're being hostile," she said.

"No, hostility would be saying something like 'Let's not blame the Cymbalta when having to spend every day with you would make any man's junk retreat into his body like a frightened animal.'"

That was the end of our relationship. She probably made some nasty notes, and then they brought in Dr. Kreigsman to give it a try. He asked permission to read my journal. Even called it a book, which I have to admit, made me kind of happy until he explained "book" was a more appropriate word for a work of fiction. We spent most of our time talking about that. What was real and what was imagined in those two months after the Internet died. I also slept. A lot. After a couple weeks, he tapered the Haldol way down, and moved me from Cymbalta to Wellbutrin, which didn't make me quite so sleepy and kept my junk in fine shape—not that I had any use for it in my time at Bellevue.

"I'm writing about my blanket," I replied, and Kreigsman smiled.

He did that a lot. Laughed at my jokes too, clearly falling into the build-self-esteem camp of shrinks. At first I resisted his attempts to butter me up, but he was just too charming. Pushing fifty and standing about five-foot-ten, with an extra twenty around the middle, he kept his clothes kind of rumpled, and didn't seem to notice that the collar of his lab coat was usually tucked under. Still, his delicate, frameless glasses were always immaculate, and sometimes he'd polish them if he needed more time to phrase his response. Once, I tried to call him out on his avuncular bluff after he told me I was obviously good to my friends.

"How could you possibly know that?" I asked.

"Well, for one," he said, nodding at the journal on my nightstand, and working his gray cloth over his lenses, "You gave Tobey all the best jokes."

I laughed, and that's how he got in, because humor's a powerful shortcut for men. We rarely just sit back and divulge, but when guys continually laugh at the same things, it means more than sharing the same sense of humor: it's sharing the same world of referential knowledge, the same moral philosophy. Your laughter acknowledges similar wiring without revealing anything.

Kreigsman took out his penlight. "Let me see your eyes for a second," he said, checking for dilation.

They did that when they pulled me from the Hudson River, too, fully dressed and soaking wet. I wasn't aware of that at the time. All I saw was a framing halo, like the camera aperture from an old-time movie. The kind that holds the action in a circle, opening to begin a story or closing at its end. And at that exact moment, I guess it was both. I could see myself on a raft, paddling west. Steady, determined strokes on a calm sea. One man with a letter close to his heart, searching for his love as he headed off into the setting sun. The end.

But the circle was opening on another story I wasn't aware of. Dr. Laurent had told me they pulled me from the water, babbling about my ex-wife, Romaya, and finding the Internet. That I had proclaimed myself the Internet Messiah, capable of returning the Net to all. I became agitated when they tried to touch my journal and violently protective of the love letter I clutched through the fabric of my breast pocket. A wet mess of angry delusions. The kind of person you sedate and commit. And that's what they did.

"Y'know," Dr. Kreigsman said, "there's nothing wrong with writing about the Internet or reading all those books on it."

Copies of *Wired* magazine flooded my nightstand, along with Blum's book, all dog-eared and highlighted. Funny that it wasn't until after my failed adventure that it first occurred to me to read about how the Internet even worked. Didn't think of it. Not even when I was walking the New York Public Library, looking for ideas.

"But," he said, "it would be great to apply all that energy to working on you."

I sat up in bed. "What more work is there? I hated my job. I missed my wife. I lost my shit when she went away. Trust me, you couldn't sit at the workers' compensation office every day without love either."

"That might be true," he said, "but there were plenty of lonely, miserable people in shitty jobs who didn't become shut-ins before suffering psychotic breaks from the loss of the Internet. Plenty of people who didn't then hallucinate friends to keep them company on New York City adventures. So, y'know, there's that . . ."

He smiled as if he'd made a joke.

"Not everything was a delusion," I said. "I went places. Met real people, too. Had experiences."

"That's true. You didn't manifest a completely fake universe, just some people. And the sooner you accept that, the sooner we can move on. I'm sure you have places you'd like to go."

He kept it vague, but it felt like a threat, or at least a bribe. He knew I still had a letter to deliver to Romaya. My initial impulse had been to feign sanity to get to California sooner, to see the wife I had imagined as dead instead of divorced, but I soon realized feigning illness would be better. That's the thing about psychiatrists, even good ones like Dr. Kreigsman: the worse your complaints, the happier they get. It gives them purpose, and if you say you have something bad and don't . . . well then, they're miracle workers, aren't they? But you still have to establish a baseline of hopelessness before they get to work.

Once I started really talking, though, I sort of lost touch with what I was pretending. I'd fallen very far from who I was, and trying to relive memories only pushed some of them further away. Often, I could only hold them like still images from childhood, like screencapped memories of late-night TV movies. But sometimes I could see the experiences from my own eyes, and that felt more legitimate. The POV became a helpful trick for sorting out the fake from the real, but just for me. For Kreigsman, I kept it mostly fake. I wasn't piecing out memories for him, just describing two months of chemically fueled fantasy.

After about two weeks, Kreigsman removed the Haldol. And after another week of me spouting like a 90's grunge song, I was ready for visitors. Not Romaya or my online buddy Tobey, who were on the other side of the country, and certainly not Oz, the wet dream of an Australian who existed mostly in my mind. But my mother.

I patted down my hair a bit and tried to sit up straight. Y'know, just the basic stuff to not look like a mental patient. No one likes their mother to see them fail. But given the hospital-issue pajamas and the fact that I was indeed in a mental health facility, my efforts weren't entirely successful. It wouldn't have mattered anyway. I could have been in a suit, sitting in a fine restaurant, and my mother would have known if something were wrong. And now, everything was wrong, so deception was just one more failure.

She didn't hug me at first, just grabbed my forearm so hard I could feel the brittle of her bones as she stared hard and quick at what had happened to her boy before the advancing tears took the clarity away.

"I'll be okay, Mom," I said.

"I know that," she said, almost angry, wiping a tear with the back of her hand. "Do *you* know that?"

She bent over and hugged me, the bed rail digging into her chest as she held me around the shoulders and kissed my cheek. Then she pulled up a chair.

"You look thin," she said.

"I'll grab a burger when they let me out."

"Are you on anything?"

"Just a low-dose of Wellbutrin," I said. "The more crazy I tell them I am, the more they lower my meds."

My mom frowned a little, and I recognized the shape of my own mouth in her face. She deserved a better joke than that. She was always funnier than the other moms, who were too busy plotting successful summer-camp strategies to crack jokes. They were like the scary ladies from the PMRC who popped up on TV, condemning Annie Lennox for androgyny while praising Michael Jackson. But music didn't make my mother nervous. She was more concerned about the agenda of women who thought it was a good idea to wear pastel, shoulder-padded suits while they all marched single file toward a better tomorrow.

When I was a kid, we watched an episode of Donahue after school where Jello Biafra of The Dead Kennedys complained that the PMRC was trying to ban their album for containing pornography. Turned out it was a reprint of an impressionist painting of male genitalia that had hung in galleries throughout Europe. "Oh, yeah?" my mother asked. "Was it well hung?" That was a big part of my mom: humor as part of a quiet, unflappable rebellion.

"How's the world doing without me?" I asked.

"The world was already living without you," she said.

"I know, but what's going on out there?"

She readjusted herself in her chair. "Your doctor asked me not to discuss it. He doesn't want you agitated."

It was true. For all his kindness, Dr. Kreigsman did not allow me television. There were many patients sicker than I who were granted that privilege, but Kreigsman believed the news and all the Apocalypse talk would only distract me from the work I had to do. "Let's worry about you," he'd say, sounding a lot more like a Jewish mother than my mom ever did.

I pressed her again. "What's going on with the Internet?"

"Who knows? You know I didn't go online even before the Apocalypse."

It was funny to hear my mother say "Apocalypse," considering she'd lost something she never really had.

"But it was back, sort of, I heard," she continued. "For a bit anyway."

"It came back?"

"Yeah, a few weeks ago. Not great, but yeah."

I sat up in bed. "Really?"

"Yeah, who's that one on MSNBC in the morning? Not him, but the woman next to him. She said that supposedly people had always been able to get on in little fits and starts around the world."

I tried to remember if I could recall a single instance of someone getting online in those two months. I flipped through my Rolodex of still images. My mother put a stop to the spinning.

"But now that's all done. It's dead. Completely. And the government is taking it over."

"Whaddya mean, taking it over? It's not a factory."

"I don't know. The . . . um. The points?"

"The hubs?"

"Yeah, hubs. I think."

A few months ago I wouldn't have known what that meant, but I'd read the books now. And although I'd never understand the science of packeted information traveling through fiber-optic cable at the speed of light, the infrastructure of the Net was still a very real and startling simple thing. Just like electricity, you still needed poles and cables to connect the world. There were only a handful of hubs on the planet—places where networks met up directly with other networks, transforming little pocketed e-villages into worldwide communities. Turns out there was one on 60 Hudson Street, walking distance from Trinity Church where I spoke to Hamilton Burke. I don't know what I would have found if I had gone there, standing outside, drunk and depressed, but I'm guessing it would have been more productive than jerking off at the Rule 34 Club for a week. Or at least productive in a way that required less cleanup afterwards.

And that was the other thing I learned in the hospital: more information about Hamilton. Obviously I knew I was speaking to a wealthy man outside Trinity Church that night, and yeah, in the back of my mind, the name was familiar. But apparently Hamilton Burke was one of the richest men on the planet. Like Warren Buffet rich. Bill Gates rich. So rich that Dr. Kreigsman didn't believe I'd met him.

"Hard to believe a man like that is just hanging out waiting to talk to you, don't you think?" he asked

"Well, he *wasn't* waiting for me. I just approached him. And is it really so weird to believe one of the richest men in the world would be in New York City's financial district?"

He let it go, but I already knew what he was thinking. Dr. Kreigsman was big on the theory that I needed to believe I was more important than I am. And certainly pretending to hobnob with the rich and powerful could support that. But why would I make that up if I didn't even know who Burke really was? And if it was wish fulfillment, why did that late-night New York City conversation fill me with such shame?

"Are you getting better?" my mother asked.

"I think so."

"So you'll go back to work?"

"Never."

For the first time, my mother sat back in her chair, pulling away from me. "Your father didn't retire until he was seventy."

"Well, I wish he would have," I said, and she came forward again until I finished my sentence. "Or would have been able to at least."

"So, no job?" she asked.

"I don't know, Ma," I said. "Dad worked to support us. To send me to college. And fucking law school, for that year anyway. I don't have those kinds of obligations."

"Well, maybe you should get some."

"Maybe," I said. "But when I get out of here, I'm going to California for a bit."

"What's in California?" she asked, but already knew. "Romaya's not your wife anymore."

"I know that."

"But isn't that the point? That you didn't know that? Didn't you forget everything?"

"She wasn't the whole problem. I hated my job, too. The job you're so eager to throw me into again."

"I don't care what job you have, I just don't want you to lie down."

"But they're paying me to. That's the whole point of disability."

"Well if you're so proud, maybe you should print up business cards."

I knew she'd disapprove, but there had to be an order for everything. It wasn't time for a job. It wasn't something I could do now.

"I just want to talk to her," I said, swapping topics in the flawed belief that I could handle the discussion. Kreigsman had already put me through the ringer about Romaya. At first he wasn't sure I was really going out West for her, considering California is also ground zero for the tech industry. What if I were continuing the investigation, and doing it on a coast that made a lot more sense than New York? But slowly he came to believe me, and even though he approved of me dealing with my mental health and emotions instead of playing Internet detective, he did not encourage that plan either.

"You're not ready for that, especially . . ." He polished his glasses again.

"They're clean," I said. "Especially what?"

"Especially if you're going to try to win her back."

"What's wrong with that?"

For the first time Kreigsman became, not angry, but more strident. "What's wrong is that you're not ready for that kind of rejection," he said. "The last time you felt it, you lost your shit. Is that clear enough for you? We've spent the last two months putting you back together. You reclaimed your identity. You want to risk all of that? Throw that all away?"

I didn't reply, and he took one more stab at it, this

time with slower and more deliberate speech. "Do you want to risk losing everything you've gained?"

I didn't answer.

"This is serious," Dr. Kreigsman said. "When you lost her, you became sheltered, delusional, dysfunctional. You lost everything."

"Well then," I said with a smile, "I must have really loved her."

But my mother didn't say any of the things Kreigsman said. She just sat there, very still, before finally speaking in a whisper.

"You can't fill someone's cup when there's a hole in it," she said.

I was defensive. Too quick to respond. "Maybe my cup has a hole in it."

"I'm sure it does," she said. "So?"

I wanted to say something about love being more like puzzle pieces, or if not puzzle pieces then maybe love was putting one cup inside another without lining up the holes, so the two cups plugged each other, but then I realized that would only hold enough water for one. So I didn't say anything. I just stayed quiet and stared a little longer. And when visiting hours were over, I felt it in her hug. The knowledge that our visit had made her no stronger. She was still carrying the weight of my hollow.

I tried to put that out of my mind for the next few days, mostly unsuccessfully. But then I caught a break to save me from contemplation. Kreigsman busted into my room with an energy I'd not seen from him before.

"It's your big day, Wayne," he said.

"You proposing?"

"Even better. I think you're ready to leave this joint."

"You're discharging me?"

"Yep."

Dr. Kreigsman handed me his clipboard, showing the order and everything.

"But I thought you were too afraid I was gonna run around being an Internet Messiah instead of doing the work that needed to be done on myself."

"I'll be honest: That remains a bit of a concern. But you've made great strides. Also, they want you out. Not all mental patients actually have an apartment to go home to."

I could visualize the period at the end of his sentence, but I also felt something more coming.

"Oh," he said, taking back his clipboard, "also there's this."

He dropped the *New York Times* on my lap. It had a banner headline: "THE INTERNET RETURNS!"

"It's back?"

"Seems so. An uninterrupted signal, at least in America, for almost two days now. Some sites still down. Sites with information housed overseas still hit or miss, but yeah, since the government took over the hubs, it's back."

"Wow."

"Yes, wow. So, y'know, investigation over, and time for you to work on you."

I jumped out of bed, grabbing my books and journal off my nightstand and shoving them into the backpack that had lived beside me for two months. It took me more time to put my shoes on than it did to pack, and that's including unzipping my Jansport to double-check that my letter to Romaya was still safely lodged in my journal.

"Doctor," I said, extending my hand. "Thank you very much."

"You're welcome. And remember, your work's just starting. Stay on your prescription, and I expect to see you in two weeks. I can refer you elsewhere, but if you don't mind, I'd like to keep seeing you for a bit."

I liked Dr. Kreigsman, but it was very important to me that I not say anything more than thank you. Really, what more was there to say? He was the best, but only on the sliding scale of incompetence representing the psychiatric profession. He hadn't fixed me. Weeks of being fed, sober, and safe fixed me. Quiet reflection on what I'd discovered on my journey fixed me. I fixed me.

"Sure," I said, putting my backpack on both shoulders, positioning my grandfather's fedora, and heading for the door.

"It's late October," he said. "You'll be cold."

I looked down at my hospital scrubs, pretending to make note of the need for warmer clothing, but that's not what I was thinking at all. I was headed someplace warm.

2.

I was too afraid to go home after the release because shutting that apartment door in Brooklyn could mean never leaving again. But it wasn't just the fear. There was nothing for me in New York. I'd hidden so completely for the last two years that the place had forgotten me. Any chance of a future was out west. I would crash with Tobey in L.A. until I got my head together. After all, it was the least he could do for me after I'd been so hospitable, even if his visit occurred only in my mind. Good friends overlooked such things.

Aside from the brown, low-top Doc Martens I was currently wearing, I left the rest of my clothes—still carrying the taint of the Hudson River—in my backpack, and opted for the style of hospital-issue, doctor-like scrubs. A sane person would have called for a ride, or at least someone to bring them clothes, but a sane person would also want to get out of a mental institution as quickly as possible. I left the hospital and took the A to JFK without a second thought. Then I bought a ticket at the airport counter just like in the movies. Disability payments had been aggregating for two months with no expenses, and still by direct deposit. It turned out to be cheaper for banks and providers to work out some system of faxing debits and credits than going back to mailing checks. Or maybe it wasn't cheaper, but the people demanded it. Also, I hadn't been paying rent. I wondered if I even had an apartment to go back to. Two months probably wasn't enough to lose the place, but I'd worry about that later. Maybe it was four months. I couldn't remember if I mailed checks during the investigation.

I wondered if the counter lady thought I was a doctor, and then I wondered what they called airport counter ladies. Cashiers? CAIRshiers? Two months earlier I would have tweeted that or hopefully let it die in my drafts folder, and that's when I realized that even though the Internet was allegedly working again, I'd made it all the way to JFK without even thinking about it. My thoughts were on Romaya, and I was proud of myself. I was calm. All the panic that had kept me indoors, kept me high, kept me manifesting delusions for company, was gone. I was outside and alone and that was okay. Although it always helped to be in transit.

The cairshier was fiddling with something below the counter instead of taking down my information.

"So," I said. "The Internet really back?"

"You haven't checked?" she asked, hurrying her iPhone into her pocket like a child busted for sneaking cookies. I tried not to notice. "Yeah, I mean, it's still all jacked," she said, "but I got on my Gmail, and BuzzFeed had some new stuff today."

"'10 Things 90s Kids Masturbated To During The Internet Apocalypse?'"

"You saw that?" she asked.

"Just a lucky guess."

She didn't believe me and it didn't matter because apparently our interaction was over. Everywhere I looked people were on their phones and laptops, but not with their typical ease. Each hit of the return button was like the pull of a slot-machine handle. Would this site work? Is there anything new? Did the e-mail fail to refresh or do I really have no messages? There were some phones for sale at an airport kiosk and if I bought one, I could get online too. I could surf the Web for the first time in two months. I could be just like everyone else. Part of them. But then I'd be here. In this airport for real. There'd be data pinning me to a place and time, and I didn't want that. I didn't want to be here. I was headed west for Romaya.

I sat on the plane, grateful for the window seat, and waited for takeoff. My companions readied their laptops and smart phones in anticipation. It would take a special kind of bastard to pride himself for not giving in to the urge to be online when only months earlier he'd been lost in years of addiction—safe, sad, and alone. But as it turns out, I was that bastard. I cracked open my *New York Times* and read about the government takeover of the hubs. Although the article didn't draw the conclusion explicitly, it seemed to me the government wasn't the culprit in the Apocalypse if removing its control from the private sector could fix the problem. But I was smart enough to know I probably didn't understand anything about the world.

My study was disturbed by the crackle of our captain over the PA, "Ladies and gentlemen, JetBlue is proud to announce that this is its first WiFi flight since the Internet Apocalypse!"

The crowd erupted into the kind of applause typically reserved for winning sports teams, and I hated myself with every fiber of my body for shaking my head with a quick laugh, like I was above such things. I forced myself to look out the window as I floated above New York and out into something undefined and blue, but really, I was counting down until the next announcement. Then it came:

"Ladies and gentlemen, JetBlue now welcomes you to use your approved electronic devices."

The laptops and phones came out from under the seats and pockets with ordered cacophony like kids taking out books from grade school desks. I watched the man next to me, a forty-something with glasses so nice you'd mistake him for a visiting European, pay his WiFi fee and get on Google. He searched "puppies" as a test run. It worked. Then, on to his Gmail. No new messages. I raised the op-ed page to obscure my spying, and he sent a test e-mail to himself, labeling it "test." (He had limited creativity.) It went through, and he made a face like a suburban dad, proud of the sauce he'd just sampled off his backyard BBQ ribs. I needed more than a newspaper to distract me from the Internet so I ordered a movie. Some high-concept comedy to hide my need.

But when the film was over, I let myself look at his laptop again. It had 25% battery life.

"Excuse me," I said. "Any chance I could use your laptop to check my e-mail? I promise I'll be off in literally two minutes."

He adjusted his glasses, running his thumb and forefinger along the arm almost all the way to his ear.

"You can watch me," I said as he considered the request. "I don't care. I just want to check."

"Just a couple of minutes," he said. "I have to do some more things before the battery dies."

I accepted this as true even though I'd already watched him refresh his Facebook three times. He turned the laptop to face me, keeping it on his fold down table. I leaned forward to sign in to my Gmail account, and he kept watch, not even pretending to hide his view of my password. I'm not sure what I was hoping to find, but I had no new messages. The last e-mails from Tobey were long since read. That's when I realized I didn't have his address. His IM light wasn't lit. No one's was. I searched my mail, looking for one with his address, and found it within twenty seconds. With that kind of efficiency, sometimes it seemed letting Google take over the world wouldn't be a bad thing. They certainly work better than the government or I.

"Almost done," I said. "Thank you."

I was done, but I wanted more playtime, and I clicked my spam folder. In it were all the typical things from Nigerian princes and black market Viagra salesmen, but there was more. There were e-mails from Romaya. E-mails from after the divorce. And they were from a normal account, which meant that if they ended up in spam it was because I'd had them automatically forwarded there to be ignored. Google helped me pretend my wife was dead instead of living without me. Apparently, there was an app for that.

I felt a tightness in my chest and it didn't come from my neighbor's oversight of my activities; it was the blackness of her unread messages waiting for me. The panic was back. I clicked the most recent e-mail. It was from several months before the Apocalypse. It was as bad as I feared. Even my neighbor, who saw everything, tried to spare me the indignity by taking off his glasses and looking away: "I understand you don't want to see me, but do me a favor and don't leave obnoxious comments on my Instagram pics. Thanks."

I signed out and thanked him, turning the laptop back in his direction.

"My ex-wife," I said, hoping that was somehow less incriminating than whatever he'd imagined.

The sky over the middle of America was just like the sky in New York and I knew it would be the same in the West. It didn't matter how quickly I traveled through it, I was reachable in a way I hadn't been in the subways. No longer safe. I closed the window shade and worked the *Times* crossword puzzle until we landed, another hour or so later. I couldn't finish it, and that felt like a bad omen for my new life. I carried those feelings with me out into LAX, looking for a sign, and short of that, a bar. I found both.

Right there in the airport, in big bold letters, was Gladstone's LAX—a seafood restaurant and bar. My journey had been preordained even if my appearance spoke equal parts doctor and mental patient. I decided I didn't want L.A. to think of me as either, so I turned my back on Gladstone's and even the alcohol inside because I needed clothes. I had some options in an airport as large as LAX, but I walked into the first store I saw.

First, I got some sandals. That seemed an obvious enough choice. My DMs weren't right for California and the sandals went just fine with the scrubs. Even made them look almost deliberately casual. I was pleased. I'd gotten really used to the comfort of scrubs and the thought of going back to real clothes wasn't particularly pleasant. I wondered if there were some other article of clothing I could get to dress them up—somehow make them more legit. That's when I saw a light, white cotton blazer, not unlike Don Johnson's old *Miami Vice* jacket. I slipped it on and it almost worked. I was getting there. The remnants of my illness mixed with L.A. airport fashion to create something new. Wasn't the way this ensemble was coming together a sign as sure as "Gladstone's"?

If I had any doubt, it soon lifted when I saw a white fedora for sale. Lighter than the somewhat traumatized fabric one I had in my hand and the perfect complement to the jacket. I walked to the store's one full-length mirror, wanting to bear witness to my own coronation as I applied the fedora. I was in white, and I felt new and clean. I took the love letter from my journal and tucked it safely into my breast pocket.

Now it was time to find Tobey. He lived in Santa Monica on Lincoln Boulevard. I thought about renting a car with GPS, but I wasn't sure GPS would be working now. I didn't want to chance it, and even with it, I didn't want to drive. At this hour, with this traffic, taking a cab seemed like a perfectly acceptable way of asking for help.

This place clearly wasn't New York, and not just because

my cabbie was Mexican, but because he was spiritually reconciled with being in traffic. That was just the deal here. But there was a bigger difference: there was no city. The 405 didn't lead to some majestic skyline that awakened possibility. It was no road to the Emerald City. It just sprawled out ahead, with only its traffic and functionality to keep it company. And as I watched the nothing go by, I thought about a story I once heard Madonna tell about when she was a fame-hungry little girl from Michigan. The day she got to New York, she asked her cabbie to take her to the middle of everything. He drove her to Times Square, and she got out amid the lights and noise and people. But that's not really a request you can make in Los Angeles. You'd need to give the driver more information, and even if you knew the location, once you got there, you'd have to be invited in. If Times Square bustles with the energy and excitement of a crowded chat room or lively comment thread, L.A. highways are the infrastructure of the Net itself: discrete passages to unremarkable locations, carrying anonymous packets of cargo.

The ride took forty-five minutes, and there was enough light left when I got there to make sure I was in the right place. I caught the complex door from a twenty-something lady walking her dog out of the building, and made my way to Tobey's apartment. It was then I realized I probably should have dropped Tobey a heads up e-mail when I was on the plane, but we'd almost never e-mailed. Ours was an IM relationship and he wasn't online when I'd checked. I needlessly consulted the address I'd scribbled on my scrap of the *New York Times* again before approaching number 19. The black plastic doorbell just below his peephole did a pretty good job of producing the sonic equivalent of a mechanical queef so I wasn't surprised when there was no answer. I knocked. Then again, but louder.

After the third knock, a voice barked out, "Come back later. Masturbating!"

The voice was definitely Tobey's.

"Jerk off on your own time," I called. "You have company."

"Who is it?" he asked, like there was a right and wrong answer to the question.

"Wayne."

"Gladstone?!"

"Yes!"

There was a pause, and then, "Come back later. Masturbating."

I heard a rustle behind the door before I could respond, and Tobey greeted me seconds later, extending his right hand for a shake.

"That's okay, tiger," I said pulling back. "I don't think you had time to wash up."

"Huh? Oh. Don't be stupid, I was joking." He grabbed my hand, shaking it vigorously and pulling me in for a hug. "Come in!"

Tobey's apartment was a lot like I'd remembered it from that one prior visit. A small perfunctory bedroom down the hall with an even smaller bathroom next to it. The main space was a living/dining room adjacent to a kitchen that was seemingly installed only to comply with a technicality in the lease. The focal point was Tobey's abused fabric couch. In front of it was a tiny glass coffee table with a laptop. A flat-screen TV hung on the opposing wall.

"Enjoy," Tobey said, placing his hand on my shoulder and gesturing to the greatness of the accommodations. "I'm having a pool put in next week."

"You're on the third floor."

"Yeah, not a big one, but deeeep."

I sat on Tobey's couch. Even my backpack was heavy enough to sink deep into its cushion. His Internet was indeed working. Also, porn was up on the screen.

"I thought you said you were joking?"

"Are you fucking kidding me?" Tobey said. "The Net's back. I hadn't jerked off to Internet porn in four months!"

I looked down at my hand.

"Don't worry. I didn't finish."

I gingerly refreshed the page just to test the connection.

"Can I get you anything?" he asked.

"Three gallons of Purell?" I replied.

The page refreshed and new girls filled the video players along the side, getting sodomized in silence. And then they froze. I refreshed again and that circle just kept turning.

"Uh, Tobes?"

"What the fuck did you do?!"

"Nothing. You saw me. I just hit refresh. Maybe they're still working the kinks out?"

"Can't believe you broke my porn," Tobey said, heading to the kitchen and grabbing us a couple of beers.

"Give it a minute," I said and accepted a can of PBR, my first drink in two months. Dr. Kreigsman noted that I'd used alcohol as a depressant, a bad way to deal with panic, but he never claimed addiction.

"So what brings you to L.A., Gladballs?"

There was a silence more awkward than the penetration I'd just witnessed, and we looked at each other. "Yeah, sorry," he said. "That sounded weird out loud."

"Yeah, save clever nicknames for IMs and texts, Tobes."

"Yarp."

"Anyway, um, this is gonna sound a little weird," I said. "But I've spent the last two months institutionalized."

Tobey could not have been less thrown.

"Did you try to kill yourself or something?"

"No, but they thought so." He just waited for more. If this were an online conversation, he would have typed "...."

"Well, I jumped off the Staten Island Ferry," I said.

"But *not* to kill yourself?"

"No, I was looking for the Internet."

I was aware none of this would make sense and I was too tired to figure out the most palatable chronological order.

"Y'know, I don't think I have the strength to go through it all again," I said. "But I did write it down. Some things are too difficult to say out loud."

"Like 'Gladballs'?"

"Exactly."

I handed Tobey my journal and he held it with more reverence than I was expecting.

"So that should explain it all, if you want to check it out while you're waiting for your porn to come back," I said.

"Answers everything, huh?"

"I think so."

Tobey looked me up and down and then back at the journal.

"One question," he asked. "Will it explain why you're dressed like an Argentinian child-prostitute pimp?"

Tobey thought it was weird to go off and read my journal in his bedroom while I sat in his apartment alone, but I insisted. It would be better to tell it all in one go, even if it meant waiting. Like taking the time for the full download instead of trying to stream and deal with the buffering. I sipped at the PBR, occasionally hitting refresh on Tobey's laptop, but mostly I just sat. It was good to sit in the world with a real person. This was a safe place. So safe I even fell asleep.

"Is the Internet back?" Tobey asked a few hours later.

I clicked refresh. "Sorry, Tobes," I said, still waking up. "No porn yet."

"Ah, that's okay. I don't need it anymore." He held up my book.

"You jerked off to my journal?"

"Oh, shut up," he said. "Like you didn't."

"What the fuck is wrong with you? That was supposed to be a chronicle of my search for the Internet."

"Yeah, nice investigation."

"Still, it wasn't meant to get you off!"

"Yeah, but Oz is hot."

I laughed. "Yeah, pretty hot."

I have a theory, and it may be self-serving, but I think you can't truly be arrogant if you can laugh at yourself, and I did laugh, because it was funny, and Tobey was funny. And laughing feels like love.

"So you gonna find Romaya?" he asked.

"That's the plan. Can I crash here for a bit?"

"After all your hospitality? Of course. I have work tomorrow, but you can borrow my car if you want."

"Work?"

"Yes, asshole. I work at the Kinkos. Well, FedEx Office now. Anyway, the point is I'm not quite the piece of shit you made me in your book."

"Sorry."

"Oh, yeah, and another thing," he said before pulling off his baseball hat. "Look."

His hair was as messy as I expected, but also jet black.

"You dyed your hair like some sort of Goth loser?" I asked.

"First of all, it's emo, not Goth, you incredibly old man, and second, no, asshole, this is my real hair color. The fuck did you make me blond in the book for?"

"Huh. Weird," I said, still seeing him as a blond. "Sorry."

"Eh, don't worry about it," he said with a wave. "You still gave me the best jokes."

3.

Sometimes, it's easy to underestimate the hospitality of the poor. Wealthy hosts offer treats, but can't match the comfort you find in a humble home where there's no fear of breaking crystal or leaving fingerprints on overly polished furniture. I lay down that night on a couch so shitty and filled with experience that I knew there was no chance of staining what wasn't mine. But sometimes influences flow the other way, and my dreams were visited by the spirits of all the nachos, beer, and bud Tobey had consumed there.

I woke almost too eager to be productive. I wanted to sit in a hard chair and work, but the work I had to do didn't involve sitting. I had to get to Romaya and I didn't even know where she was. I mean, she wasn't hiding from me. I had a forwarding address somewhere at home maybe. If I hadn't thrown it out, which I probably had. I didn't keep a spam folder for unpleasant reminders in real life. I hit refresh on Tobey's laptop again, and this time the silent naked women in the margins started to animate. If I wanted, there was an "amazing penetration" embedded in the middle of the screen, all teed up for viewing.

But like any stalker or cut-rate private eye, I went to Spokeo and typed in Romaya's name. Then her maiden name. And there she was. In L.A. A fractured image returned to me, but it wasn't like a reclaimed memory. Just information I knew existed somewhere, untethered to anything concrete. The computer screen was shedding faint light on details left in the dark to starve and die.

MapQuest told me that she was in Brentwood, only four miles away, and seeing the partial street name reminded me it was an address I'd seen before. I didn't need to pay Spokeo the fee for her full information because I remembered now. 59572 Gorham Ave.

It was 6:38 a.m. Given L.A. traffic, I figured there might be enough time to get to her before she went to work. I wrote down the directions, knowing there was no chance of Tobey having a printer, and then carried his now-working laptop to his room so he'd have it when he awoke. Tobey was sleeping on his stomach, hugging his pillow, and his legs were bent at the knees with his feet in the air. I snapped a picture with his laptop like those ridiculous N.Y.C. tourists who take pics with their tablets. Once his stupidity was captured, it also became important to document it, and for the first time since the Apocalypse, I posted something to Facebook. "I just arrived, but does everyone in L.A. sleep like an asshole here or just my buddy Brendan Tobey?" Then I pushed down hard on his arm.

"Wake up," I said.

Tobey was startled. "What?!"

"Nothing. You're sleeping like an asshole."

"What?"

"Well look at you," I said. "Who sleeps like that?"

Even I couldn't believe how annoying I was being, and I wondered if maybe more of Tobey's spirit had entered during my sleep than I'd imagined.

"Sorry," I said. "I just need your car keys. . . . but you do sleep like an asshole."

Tobey pointed to his desk where I saw his keys and Altoids box of weed resting on top of my journal.

"Now, leave me alone," he said. "I'm not getting up 'til 8:45."

"Won't you miss work?" I asked.

"Nah, I can leave later. I'm walking."

I went to take back the journal.

"Could you do me a favor and leave that?" he asked. "It's boring at work."

"There are other books you could read."

"See any in this apartment?"

I found some unused wire hangers in Tobey's hall closet and hung my clothes in the bathroom before taking a shower. Not quite like doing laundry, but I hoped the steam would at least get rid of the wrinkles. I suppose I could have borrowed some of Tobey's clothes, but his legs were longer, and I thought it was unlikely he owned anything other than profanity-riddled T-shirts.

Before leaving, I made sure my letter to Romaya and

directions were both still in the inside jacket pocket of my L.A. ensemble. I knew I'd need to get clothes at some point and wondered whether there was a Target, or at least a medical supply store, in the neighborhood. When I got down to the garage level I realized I'd forgotten to ask Tobey what he drove, but the '01 Toyota Matrix parked right across from the staircase door looked familiar. Another clue was the dirty laundry pressed against the back glass and the bumper sticker for VaginalBlood Fart.com—his failed start-up that never progressed beyond the merchandizing phase.

Tobey's car drove well enough, but as I made my way to Brentwood, I became painfully aware that I had no firm comprehension of what "L.A." was. How could a cobbling of suburbs be a city? And wasn't Santa Monica, where I was coming from, its own thing? I wasn't sure and I guess it didn't matter if I understood unless I was staying. I pulled over when I reached Gorham Avenue and parked outside the building that my piece of paper said was Romaya's. I stared at the rows of two- or four-unit apartment buildings, one right after another, all with garages. I'd never understand this place.

It was 7:53 and I thought about knocking on Romaya's door, but I needed to see her first. Or at least I wanted to. I sat watching the garage, hoping the Prius was hers, and wondering if she could really afford it. I was nervous I'd already missed her, but not so nervous that I got out and rang her bell.

At 8:15, she came out, wearing slacks and a blouse like a full-blown businessperson. She was still fit and her dark brown hair was tied up into the same functional bun like it usually was for work, but she was different.

She moved like a woman, knowing where she was going, undeterred by daydreams. I watched her fumble for her keys from behind the safety of a framed glass window. And then, just like that, she drove away. Fear had cost me my chance to make this less awkward. With no cell phone or e-mail, how was I to tell her I was coming? I was forced to surprise her, and that was okay. But now I was following her, and there was no way to pretend that didn't look creepy.

The traffic meant it took twenty-five minutes to go about three miles before we arrived at a nondescript office building in some town that may or may not have still been Brentwood. I'd seen L.A. traffic before, but this was worse. The city had still not compensated for all the traffic signals controlled online, and many intersections still relied on police personnel pulling traffic duty to get the cars where they needed to go. When we reached our destination, I saw the parking lot was lined with palm trees along one side. I parked first so I could exit my car while Romaya was still in hers. After another thirty seconds, she got out, swiping at her iPhone in frustration. Something was wrong. Soon I would say hello and then there would be two things.

"Babe," I called out.

She flipped around, doing a whiplash inspection for the sound so quickly, she passed right over me before returning to see what she'd overlooked. I waved. She didn't speak, and I stepped into the silence.

"Hello," I said, now only a few steps away.

I saw the word "Babe" form behind her lips, but she didn't speak, and when we were close enough to touch, she didn't touch. She just said "What?" almost involuntarily. Nothing made sense, and although a warmer greeting would have been welcomed, it was fun to see her revert back to her younger self as she was thrown out of the familiar and into the new.

"Hi," I said again, and placed my hands gently on her shoulders before leaning in for the politest of kisses on her cheek. For a dead woman, she smelled great, and a thousand tiny hands poured from me, swiping desperately at her wafting pheromones without a trace of dignity. I used to kiss her at the very top of her cheekbone where those scents lived, over and over, soft and tender, and I never had to stop because something entered me with each kiss. Something that grew and floated up into another. I leaned in again to kiss her correctly, but saw the faintest flake of dry skin around her earlobe piercing and remembered how toward the end, the kisses went out like ripples on a pond, expanding further and further without return.

"Why are you dressed like that?" she asked.

"Like what?"

"I don't know," she said. "Sonny Crockett's podiatrist?"

I didn't have a succinct explanation, but it was a fairly rhetorical question.

"Sorry," she said. "It's just I'm incredibly late." She looked at the entrance of the building. "What are you doing here?"

"Visiting Tobey," I lied. "But I wanted to see you."

Romaya accepted the answer easily, the way you do with strangers in an elevator, when you won't be around long enough to disagree. But then she didn't.

"Why now?" she asked, and I remembered there was a time when a visit would have seemed less strange. She'd

wanted to see me when she returned to New York to fi-
nalize the divorce, months after she'd left, but I insisted
all communications go through lawyers. I signed the papers in a shitty little office on Court Street and avoided
her during the stay. I didn't want to see her look at me
as something other than her husband. Things got cloud-
ier after that.

"Why now?" she repeated.

But I didn't answer because "I'm ready now" wasn't
an answer.

"Can we talk when you're done with work?" I asked.

"I'll have to call you," she said. "I don't know when
I'm getting off."

"I didn't bring my phone. I haven't used it since the
Apocalypse."

That felt good to say. I wanted her to know.

"Doesn't matter," she said, holding up her iPhone. "It's
out again. That fix didn't last long."

"I could meet you here at, I don't know, six, seven?"
I offered.

"I'm usually done by seven, but I can't promise. If I
can't get out, I'll come out then and tell you, okay?"

She was already turning toward the entrance when I
said, "Okay, Romaya."

" 'Romaya' sounds weird," she said.

"Would you prefer Babe?" I asked.

"Probably not."

"Hmm," I scratched my chin. "What if I lose the hat?"

"You're still funny," she said without laughing and
hurried in to work. "So late."

I sat in the parking lot because there was nowhere I
needed to go. A few landscapers worked on a row of palm

trees, getting rid of all the dead brown leaves and over-growth, ensuring the trees maintained their cartoon appearance. Soon the parking lot would be fenced in with perfect, brown, swirly sticks inserted into green pom-poms. Such a ridiculous city. They worked diligently, making their way toward my car, tree by tree, until everything less than perfect had fallen to the ground. When it was over, the head guy, taller and more slender than the other two, took a step back to survey the work, standing an arm's length from my open car window.

"Nice job," I said.

"Oh, didn't see you," he said with a start, and then followed with a more conversational, *"Gracias."*

"Yeah, very pretty."

"Ah, fuck pretty," he said. "Keeps the rats away."

"What?"

"Yeah, they nest up there unless you shave them."

"Rats nest in palm trees?" I asked.

"Yeah, you didn't know that?"

"I'm not from around here. In New York, we keep our rats in the subway."

"Yeah, well welcome to L.A., *amigo.*"

I watched him get in his truck while his crew hopped in the back along with all the underbrush I hoped had been cut before nesting. They drove away, and I considered doing the same because it didn't matter if I had nowhere to go, I couldn't wait here until seven. But then I heard a crash followed by what sounded like Romaya screaming, "Fuck!"

I ran to the sound and saw her bending over a cardboard box of books and spilled papers. Her trunk was open. As I got closer, I saw a broken picture frame on the ground. She was pulling her papers out from underneath it, taking care not to be cut by the scattered shards.

"What happened?" I asked.

"They fired me," she said.

"For being late?"

"No for . . . well, y'know, they didn't really say. But I'm fired."

"I'm sorry, Babe," I said without thinking. She didn't seem to mind.

"Fuckers did it by e-mail," she said, putting the last of her papers in the box.

Now, all that was left was the shattered frame. The picture, a photo of her under a giant redwood tree, had been scratched by the glass.

"I've had that frame since my first job," she said.

Behind the damaged tree photo was another picture I recognized, and I slowly pulled it out, letting the top photo act as a buffer against all that was sharp and damaging. It was our wedding photo.

"Well at least this is still safe," I said, handing it to Romaya.

She looked down at the redwood photo instead, so I handed that to her too while I piled the glass slowly with the side rubber of my sandal. Then I took a manila folder from her box and got most of it on there before encasing it with a reverse flip. I folded the top and sides over.

"A little care package of glass," I said. "Want me to deliver it to your old boss?"

"I didn't even get the e-mail," she said. "They sent it as soon as the Net came back last night, and when I walked in they're looking at me like, 'oh, hey, uh, ... aaahhhh, hmmm.'"

"Ouch."

"And I'm such an idiot. It took me forever to get it. They're all like 'oh, after the e-mail, we didn't expect to see you . . . .'"

"Painful."

"Yeah. So I'm just standing there silent, and Ken, that's my boss, is like, 'Well, um, we sent you an e-mail last night. . . .'"

"Did they give you severance?" I asked, and she laughed. "What? No severance?" I asked.

"No, that's the best part. I went to my desk because we can still get internally sent e-mail with this anti-quated makeshift thing they did and they gave me two weeks!"

"That's pretty shitty after two years."

"Yeah, but I only found that out later because when they told me, when they actually had to see me, when I was in their face crying and packing up this box of shit, they were like, 'Forget the e-mail. We know times are tough,' and they gave me three months!"

"Awesome. That's like free money!" I said, but it wasn't what she wanted so I tried again. "I guess they realized you're a much better employee in person."

She was happier with that.

"Fuckers," she said.

"Yeah," I agreed, and she smiled. "We were always good at hating other people, weren't we?" I asked, but she turned to shut her trunk and I jumped like a commuter for a closing subway door.

"Hold on," I said. "There's something else that belongs with your things."

The love letter was in my jacket pocket, folded in four

as it had been before, when it sat in our closet for two years, but it was no longer a relic. Now it carried the experiences of my New York investigation, and traces of the Hudson River. It had the memories of sitting watch over me while I healed up in the hospital. It had the knowledge, by osmosis, of all the books stacked on top of it as it dried. It was waiting for release and now it wanted home.

I took out the letter and offered it to Romaya.

"What's that?" she asked.

"It's yours."

She held the letter only with her fingertips, fearful that full contact would mean acceptance, and unfolded it no more than necessary before sealing it up again.

"I gave this back to you," she said, holding it in front of her.

"I don't want it. It's yours."

Romaya closed her trunk and readied her keys. "I can't," she said, and placed it back into my jacket pocket. It would have been too childish to run away like a game of tag, and the feel of her fingers across my chest also made it hard to move.

"Thank you," she said, pushing the letter into place and taking, instead, the package of broken glass. She got into her car and I watched her wave in the rearview mirror without turning around, the way you thank another motorist who makes an opening that lets you go on your way.

A normal man would have taken that as a cue for adventure. Explored California, untied to anything, but the thought of getting lost in traffic was too much to bear. I headed home past the newly shaved palm trees and the row of stupid apartment buildings I'd seen before until I reached Romaya's apartment and reversed my handwritten MapQuest directions. When I got home, Tobey's space was still waiting, and I parked like the last hour had never even happened. I didn't know where I was going, but I was sure I'd find something to occupy me before dissolving into Tobey's couch for the rest of the day. I wound up at a miserable sports bar somewhere along what they called the promenade. Apparently, sports fans drink Budweiser in Santa Monica too, and I ordered one because there was a special. Then I ordered two because the first went down like water that was bad for you and I still didn't want to go home. The next one was a buyback, and even in a shitty Santa Monica sports bar, the bartender said, "This one's on the house, buddy," because some things just need to be the same everywhere.

"Thanks man," I said, and he smiled in a way that made it easy to picture his headshot from twenty years earlier.

Although the bar was filled with SportsCenter plasma screens, one lone, poorly-placed TV was showing MSNBC with the sound off and subtitles on. The news told me what I already knew: The Net was out again. Unofficial comments from the White House made only vague references to the problem being more systemic and complicated than first thought. Apparently, the Apocalypse was engineered by more than just some bumpkin leaning against the wrong switch at the hubs. But I wasn't much in the mood for believing anything. And it wasn't even politics or a question of trust. This was an administration that couldn't get its healthcare Web site working. At the end of the day, it doesn't matter what field you're talking about, only about three percent of people are good at their job, and that's just not enough manpower to fix the world's problems.

After several rounds of wings, I finally left the bar, beer-tired but sober. When I reached Tobey's door, I heard music coming from inside, which was good because it wasn't until that moment that I realized I didn't have keys to his place. I knocked, but had trouble making myself heard over Yes' *Awaken*. Tobey finally came to the door, eyes bloodshot and weary, but happy, as he took a step back to reveal all of his apartment. The stink of shwag wafted into the hall, but I was more preoccupied by the man on the couch—a fifty-something sporting a balding ponytail and a *Doctor Who* T-shirt so stiff and new it looked like it still reeked of silk screen.

"Gladstone!" Tobey exclaimed, pointing to the couch. "You know this dude?"

I studied him for a moment, tilting my head to make sure what I was seeing was really there. "Well, let me ask you, is this dude a fifty-something man with a pony tail and *Doctor Who* T-shirt?" I asked.

"Uh, yeah?"

I heard myself say "Jeeves," but I didn't really say anything, because how do you greet something you don't understand? I had been positive Jeeves was real when I first got to the hospital because I had clear memories of the man who sat at his little table in Central Park, working as a human search engine, selling information to people too lazy to open books for free. But after that the memories got hazier, and when he never came to see me, I started to believe he wasn't real.

"Gladstone?" he asked.

"Jeeves?"

He planted his palms on his knees and sprang from the sinkhole of Tobey's couch with more grace than I expected. "Yes!"

"Come in," he said, and I wondered why I needed to be invited into my own friend's home by a more comfortable stranger. I took only a few slow steps before he came over and put his arm around me, leading me to the couch.

"It's good to see you," he said. "Why are you dressed like that?"

"Like what?"

"I dunno . . ."

"An Argentinian child-prostitute pimp?" Tobey offered.

"No," Jeeves replied. "I was gonna say something like a back-alley Monte Carlo plastic surgeon?"

"Too wordy," I said.

"Definitely," Tobey agreed.

"Well, anyway, it's great to see you."

Jeeves plopped back into the couch, and I took a seat as Tobey went off to the kitchen.

"So," Jeeves said. "What have you been up to?"

"Well, I just got in yesterday. Catching up with Tobey. Trying to reconnect with my ex."

I could see Jeeves lose his energy.

"No," he said. "I meant about the Internet. Your investigation."

"I don't have an investigation."

"Of course you do! You're the Internet Messiah, remember?"

I hadn't heard that phrase in a couple of months and

it embarrassed me to remember I'd written that about myself. It was more cringe-worthy than a three-quarter head-turn selfie, shot from above.

"Holy shit, that messiah shit's real?" Tobey asked, returning with two PBRs. "I thought Gladstone was just blowing himself again."

"Yes, it's real," Jeeves said.

"This guy's gonna find the Internet?" Tobey said, pointing to me with one PBR while extending the other to Jeeves. "Says who?"

"Says me." Jeeves grabbed Tobey's wrist with his left hand, removing the beer with his right. Then he laid his palm flat on top of Tobey's.

Tobey pulled away after a few seconds. "Bad touch, Mr. Grabby."

Jeeves made a pronouncement. "Three things: First, you're not my type. I like my men able to speak in full sentences. Second, this morning you jerked off to a Web site called 'Amazing Penetrations,' and third . . ." Jeeves looked down at his hand. "Do you have any Purell?"

Tobey was impressed. Shocked, even. I'd never seen him lose his flippancy before. He seemed to search for it on the floor as he took a seat.

Jeeves was here so either I was in a fully psychotic state right now or I was less crazy than I thought. He was the man I remembered. A man full of information, both learned and divined. But something still wasn't right.

"Jeeves," I asked. "If you really believe that, that I was this Internet Messiah . . ."

"Am," he corrected. "Yes?"

"Why didn't you visit me? I sat in Bellevue for two months. You never came once."

"You weren't allowed visitors. Didn't you know that?"

"My mother came."

"Immediate family only. I tried. Repeatedly."

"I'm sorry," I said. "It's just I've been trying to put together a lot of what happened during those two months. I was told most of it was fake."

"Fake?"

"Well, y'know . . . delusional." It didn't feel good to say, but I could see that Jeeves was so sure of his messianic pronouncement that he would need convincing.

"Gladstone, I met you in Central Park," he said, almost angrily. "I found you in your hotel. Those memories are real."

"Yeah, well did you also appear with Agent Rowsdower at a press conference when I was declared a person of interest under the NET Recovery Act?"

"No . . ."

"Yeah, well in my mind you did. That was real to me. As real as those other things. I wrote it down."

"Paranoia. The weed, the drink, the anxiety . . ."

"I don't need a diagnosis, Jeeves. I need to know what happened, and I've spent two months reconstructing memories where I was nothing important. Where I was just sad, Internet-addicted, and alone. I can deal with that. It's embarrassing, but I can accept it. But now you're fucking it all up again."

"So everything was a psychosis? You dreamed you were the Internet Messiah like some batshit loony? Do you really think you could fall so far?"

"I *did* fall so far! I jumped off the Staten Island Ferry!"

"Yeah, that made the paper, but you were high. You were depressed."

"Again, stop diagnosing. I wasn't suicidal. In my mind, I was paddling my raft to the Statue of Liberty, looking for the Internet."

That finally put Jeeves off his game, and it was good to see him without answers for once. He stared at me, confused, as the remnants of my anger settled about the room. Then Tobey came to the rescue.

"Y'know, Jeeves," Tobey said, holding up my journal, "you should really just read the book. It's all right here."

"Book?" Jeeves asked.

"Not a book," I said, snatching it back from Tobey. "A journal. And it's mine."

"Gladstone's right," Tobey said, picking his backpack up off the floor, "but here, take one of these." He pulled out one of several clipped bundles of paper and handed it to Jeeves. "I made copies."

"Why?" I asked."

"Whaddya mean why? I work at Kinko's."

"Yeah, but why make copies of my book?"

"Because I wanted my own. And Steve wanted to read it too, once I told him what it's about, and some of my jokes."

"*My* jokes," I said. "I wrote it."

"Yeah, but my delivery was spot-on."

"You're such a prick, Tobey."

"Oh, and then I made a few for the guys in shipping."

"Anyone else?"

"Taheesha. Well, all the cashiers, really."

I just waited.

"Oh, and this really hot chick who came in to buy an insane amount of bubble wrap."

"Good," I said. "For a second, I was afraid not everyone in the state of California was going to be aware of how much I masturbated during the Apocalypse."

Jeeves was taking his time to flip through the pages of my book. I liked the way he touched them, folding back the page halfway, then pushing it over. There was care and respect. I felt the need to explain.

"I started out keeping it like a chronicle of the Apocalypse. Then some details of the investigation, but, ultimately, it just documented what became of me."

"Well, I'll take a look," he said. "Maybe I can verify some things for you."

"Wait a second," Tobey said. "If you've never read that, how did you even know who I am? How did you find me?"

Jeeves closed the book. I was pretty sure I knew what he was going to say and I beat him to it.

"What part of psychic don't you understand?" I asked.

"Well, no," Jeeves said. "I was already in L.A. for a comic convention. I was supposed to leave today, but then I saw your Facebook posting this morning."

"We're not Facebook friends," I said. "We met during the Apocalypse."

"Yes, but I followed you when it came back, and your statuses are public because you're a dirty attention whore."

"What status?" Tobey asked.

"I took a picture of you sleeping like an asshole this morning," I said.

"Right," Jeeves continued. "And he tagged you in it.

So then I went to your page, and I found out your employer, and then found you at the store, and you know the rest."

"So, it was just a simple online investigation that any preteen could do that helped you find me?" Tobey asked. "Not special powers?"

Jeeves smiled. "Yes, but, y'know, that's still pretty special, right?" Then he looked to me. "We need you, Gladstone."

"We!" I laughed. "Who? It's great to see you, really, but seriously."

"It's not just me. Anonymous was asking about you too."

"Get the fuck out," Tobey said.

"I'm serious," Jeeves insisted. "He had a mask and everything."

"Did he call himself, what was that name from the book again?" Toby asked. "Quiffmonster42?"

"Uh, no," Jeeves said. "I just told you he was from *Anonymous* . . ."

"Well, in Tobey's defense," I said, "I went to a 4Chan meet up, and trust me, in real life you have to call a room full of twats *something*."

"Isn't that a gaggle?" Toby offered. "A gaggle of twats?"

Jeeves wasn't amused. "No, he didn't give a name. And I had nothing to tell him anyway. I hadn't seen you. I couldn't get to you."

"Fair enough," I said, hoping to end the discussion, and failing.

"And now that I've found you, I don't know what you're doing."

"I'm enjoying freedom," I said. "Seeing old friends. And trying to get my wife back."

"She's not your wife anymore, dude," Tobey said.

"I know. I'm working on it."

Jeeves had a mission, but he wasn't impractical or unkind so he let it drop for the moment. "So lads," he said. "I changed my flight and it's not 'til tomorrow. What would you like to do? My treat."

Tobey was quick with a suggestion. "Let's go to The Hash Tag. We can catch the early show."

"What's that?" I asked.

"Just a place down on Main Street. They play hashtag games."

Jeeves and I looked at each other.

"You know," Tobey continued, "like on Twitter. They come up with funny hashtag topics posted up on a screen and then you write funny responses. There are prizes."

"You mean like #FirstWorldProblems and things like that?" Jeeves asked.

"Yeah, but not old and lame," Tobey replied. "I love it."

It seemed innocuous enough, and Jeeves was happy to oblige, so we took Tobey's Matrix. I let Jeeves ride shotgun, and I packed myself into the backseat.

From the outside, The Hash Tag was like any other dingy bar, but the sign was new and bright neon pink. Inside, it was dark, but I could make out a series of small tables, each replete with a hookah and bong. The air hung thick with what I assumed was official California-issue medical marijuana.

"This is a drug den!" I said.

"Duh," Tobey replied. "Why do you think they call it The *Hash* Tag?"

"Because they play hashtag games you said."

Tobey considered that for a moment. "Well, yeah, but why do you think I said I loved it?"

We found a table about halfway back and to the side, and a waitress with several face piercings came over a minute later with clean mouthpieces for our hookah.

"Welcome to The Hash Tag," she said. "Have you been here befo—oh hi, Tobey!"

"Hi Jynx," he said. "These are my friends Jeeves and Gladstone. Jeeves is a psychic and Gladstone jumped into the Hudson River to find the Internet."

Even a girl with blue hair, safety pins in her face, and a "backless" ripped T-shirt thought Tobey was a weirdo.

"Okay . . . well, here's your paper and pencils. We're gonna start up the first show in a few minutes."

"Thank you," I said. "Could I get a Jameson on the rocks?"

"Oooh, sorry," she said. "Our liquor license got temporarily suspended. We just have beer. Can I get you anything else?"

"Three PBRs," Tobey said.

"Uh, actually," Jeeves interrupted, "We'll take three Anchor Steams."

"Okay, great." Jynx wrote the order down, seeming to know she wouldn't remember. "And can I offer you any flavored tobaccos?

"We're good," Tobey said, patting the backpack he'd brought with him.

"Okay, I'll be back with those beers." She turned to go.

"And some water," I said, glimpsing her back tattoo of the dragon dog from *The NeverEnding Story,* intersected by a maroon bra. "She's totally not bringing that water," I grumbled to Tobey.

"Don't be so pessimistic," he said, taking his box of Altoids from his backpack. "Jynx is great."

"Hey," Jeeves asked, "how did you know I wouldn't have preferred some flavored tobacco?"

"How did you know I didn't prefer PBR? Besides," Tobey said, opening up the box to reveal a full stash, "this *is* flavored. Curiously strongly flavored."

Tobey packed his weed into the hookah before fitting three of the tubes with mouthpieces. Then Jynx came back with the beers and a pitcher of water.

"See?" Tobey was gloating.

"Here are your Anchor Steams."

"Thanks Jynx," Tobey said.

"And here's your water."

"Thank you," I said, before watching Jynx fill the bong and head back to the bar.

"Hmm . . . technically, I still won that bet," Tobey said.

The night went pretty much the way you'd expect. They'd announce a game, some stupid hashtag like #WorstThingAboutFirstTimeSex (Eve is selfish in bed) or #FilmPrequels (*Honey, I Think We Should Have Kids*), and they'd give prizes for the best one in each round, usually in the form of free food or beer or tobacco. We had a good enough time, but it was starting to bother me that we hadn't won yet.

"Well, if you want to win," Tobey said, "you have to know how to play the room. You published at *McSweeney's*, you get it," he said.

"Okay," Jynx said, stepping on the six-inch-high pallet that served as a stage. She was now wearing a T-shirt based on Magritte's *Son of Man*, but instead of an apple in front of his face, there was a WiFi symbol. "This is the final hashtag of the early show," she said. "The winner gets one free beer and this T-shirt." Jynx proceeded to take off the shirt, revealing that ornate, maroon bra underneath and enough tattoos to never be naked. The crowd cheered and wolf-whistled, but in the way friends and gay men do at burlesque shows where you're sure it's safe and no one's getting raped.

"Okay, your final category is #21stCenturyYoMommaJokes. Go!"

Tobey hookah'd it up while Jeeves sat back pondering and scratching at his stubble. I looked at Jynx and, remembering Oz, had the scary thought that maybe she wasn't real. Tobey scribbled "Yo' Momma so dumb, she consults WebMD for a computer virus." Tight. Jeeves took a little too much pride in his submission as he slid his paper across the table for view: "Yo' Momma so boring, the NSA didn't even read her e-mail." That wouldn't win. This was a crowd that liked LOL funny and would always give wry second place unless it was wry mixed with the absurd.

"Times almost up, Gladdy," Tobey said. Jynx was already collecting the slips.

"I got it," I said, handing my paper directly to Jynx while doing a sensational job of maintaining eye contact.

"Cool hat," she said, and headed for the stage.

Somehow, I knew I'd won it, just like I knew back in college that I was going to win a complimentary copy of *Speed* at my college-town video store when I dropped my name in a box. It was only the second time in my life I'd felt something so strongly. I had a superpower, but only for things of no consequence. Tobey's and Jeeves' submissions got laughs, but mine did better: "Yo' Momma so gay she can get married in an increasing number of states."

"It's Gladstone, right?" Jynx asked the crowd, but didn't wait. Instead, she came over to me with the cheers at her back and took off my hat before placing it on her head. "Time to claim your prize," she said. I took off my *Miami Vice* jacket, revealing the scrubs underneath. "Here you go, Doctor," she said, pulling the T-shirt over my head before returning my hat. "Perfect." I couldn't remember the last time I'd been dressed by a woman. Then she hurried back to the stage.

"Tobey, help me out here," I said. "Is she . . ."

"Real?" he asked.

"Yeah."

"Of course she is. Don't be so surprised. Not every Suicide Girl is all doom and gloom."

"Yeah, but I think she . . . likes me."

Jynx returned to the stage and said, "Thank you all for playing, and remember, you can buy that T-shirt and others at my boyfriend's site. ThisFuckinShirt.com. I mean, when the Net comes back."

"Don't worry about it," Tobey said. "She was too tall for you anyway."

"Tall chicks dig me," I said. "They're looking down from above. It's a slimming perspective."

Our strong finish and Tobey's winning personality had brought people (some of them women) to our table, but I wasn't looking for company. Neither Jynx nor any of these Californians were my type, or the woman I'd crossed the country and feigned sanity to see. I also wasn't in a position to be the wingman Tobey wanted. My thoughts were on Romaya, so Tobey used me in book form, pulling copy after copy of my journal out of his backpack and giving them away.

After about thirty minutes of downing Anchor Steams on Jeeves' tab, someone made a plan to go the movies, specifically, the ELO-scored Olivia Newton-John vehicle *Xanadu*. Tobey and Jeeves argued first about whether it was a good bad movie or a bad good movie, but I couldn't really follow. Winning that shirt made me feel special, and I let myself think about all the things Jeeves had told me back at the apartment. And maybe because I was in no shape to, I started putting together the pieces of a new reality. One that had more parts than I'd been accepting. Back in college, Romaya had a poetry professor who would cut up students' poems without mercy, chopping away all the pretense and bombast and leaving only those phrases that worked. I could see the value in that, but she hated it. Why not teach us to write the bigger poem we're failing at, she asked. Build a better home instead of trapping us into one tiny, immaculate room?

I realized that Dr. Kreigsman had done that to my life—reduced it to a simple story that worked and made sense, but could never capture all the moving parts and ill-fitting corners of a real existence. There was more. But even harder than figuring out what was real was deciding if certain memories were worth the risk of reclaiming. After all, there are worse things than an immaculate room.

Tobey and Jeeves ultimately agreed *Xanadu* was a good bad movie, but there was no meeting of the minds as to whether the soundtrack could be called progressive rock. Jeeves had solid points against such a classification: no odd time signatures, no extended solos, and of course, the presence of Olivia Newton-John. Wisely, Tobey countered with, "Yeah, but robot voices and laser sounds!" I tried not to fill my head with too much of it. I couldn't even comprehend what theatre would be showing a 1980 film today, but apparently, it was Hollywood Forever—a graveyard that projected films upon a mausoleum wall while spectators watched picnic style. And although it sounded like it, this was no apocalyptic creation. Hollywood Forever predated the Internet, and it sounded great, but I declined because proximity to Jeeves would only invite further conversation I wasn't ready for.

I pulled Jeeves away from the crowd. "Bring it in here, big guy," I said, and wrapped my arms around him. And when he grabbed me too hard and placed his chin over my shoulder there was some part of me that wanted to cry.

"Thank you, Daniel," I said. "I'll friend you on Facebook when the Net comes back, and let you know when I'm back in New York."

He pulled back from the embrace and held me close at the elbows. I noticed for the first time that he had really long eyelashes that actually made contact with his glasses. "First, it's Dan, never Daniel, and second, I don't see it coming back without you, Gladstone."

"I'm a mess, Dan."

"I know, but you'll get stronger."

"Oh, did you have a vision of that?"

He smiled. "You don't have to be psychic. Everyone who keeps going gets stronger." He took a piece of paper out of his pocket, put it in my hand and kept it there. "This is my number. A landline."

"I'll miss you."

"You'll see me again, Gladstone. Just, y'know, keep going."

I made no promises. I just watched him join Tobey and the gang as they headed off to a cemetery to see a movie about roller skating muses. I stopped Tobey long enough to tell him I'd see him later and score one of the copies of my journal for myself. Then I called a cab to take me back to that sports bar in Santa Monica, the only bar I knew. I was hoping to read the journal's words again, this time as if they weren't mine. To use my newly formed mind to separate facts from disease.

"You're back," the bartender said, as I reclaimed my stool from the afternoon.

"Maybe," I said, and asked for two fingers of The Macallan.

It was meant to be a reward. Two months of drinking out in the world of New York City had forced me to seek booze from a lower shelf. It had been Jameson over and over and that was okay. I liked Jameson fine, and even though it was Irish whiskey, it actually tasted more like The Macallan than some lesser Scotches I'd tried. But now, I felt I'd earned the real thing. Not just with those two months of hospital-based sobriety or the couple of days of occasional cheap beer at Tobey's, but because I had important things to consider. Scotch things. Beard-stroking, pipe-smoking things.

The bartender got distracted by a large party of people crowding up against the bar, and I flipped through the Tobey-printed copy of my journal while I waited. He'd written "Gladstone" in the bottom right corner and beneath that "Illustrations by Brendan Tobey." I was instantly pissed off that the fucker had doodled all through my book, but as I turned the pages, I noticed really only a handful of drawings, and all of them good. He'd used a fine felt pen and scratched out sketches on inserted pages in a kind of style that married a *New Yorker* cartoon with a dime-store noir novel. Back at the workers' compensation office, people referred to such efforts as "adding value to the team."

The bartender brought my Macallan on a napkin. A nice coaster would have been more fitting, but at least the place was relatively quiet for a sports bar. I took a slow sip, letting the ice stop at my teeth and the Scotch flow underneath. The smoke and warmth I'd remembered were almost there, but cut by a medicinal taste that distracted me. I'd forgotten how to drink good Scotch. My brain focused on the wrong things. The months of Jameson had left their mark. Going cheap had ruined me.

4.

What came next should have arrived in a day, but it took a week. Every morning I woke and got dressed in some incredibly stylish number I'd picked up from Old Navy and went outside with the intent of continuing on to Romaya. But I didn't want to see her again with a tightness in my chest. The gasping in my lungs could turn to hurt and then anger if not met with comfort. I waited each day to feel good, but I never felt good. But not all decisions are fated—some are just overdue. So one week after seeing her for the first time in L.A., I made myself see her again.

I knew you couldn't hail a cab here, even if people like to pretend L.A.'s a real city, so I headed to the promenade where tourists being dropped off for shopping meant there might be one around. The taxi would get me to Romaya, and when I arrived, I'd have to get out because I wouldn't be allowed to hide behind someone else's metal and glass.

There was no text, no IM, no Facebook message. Romaya didn't know I was coming, and there was no reason for her to be home. Maybe I was counting on that. A knock on an empty door. But she was home even if her greeting wasn't everything I'd hoped for.

"What are you doing here?" she asked. I saw some panic I didn't accept.

"I'm sorry. Is it a bad time?" I asked.

"No. . . . No," she said. "I'm just working on my résumé and looking for a job. Would you like to come in?"

"Thank you." I stepped inside. It didn't smell like our old apartment. "I got you something," I said, and pulled a picture frame from my Jansport. It was like the one she'd broken. I picked it up from CVS on one of the days I couldn't bring myself to visit her.

"Oh. Thank you," she said.

Her futon was nicer than the one we used to call our bed, but not as nice as something I expected a grown-up to keep in her living room. It had a crafty, hippie, knit blanket-rug-shawl thing draped over it to class it up. I sat down and stared at her tiny dining room table with actual newspapers spread out across it.

"Wow," I said. "That's fun."

"Yeah, classifieds."

Romaya continued to make the coffee she had started before I got there. "They say you can pay a fee to Monster.com and they will do searches for you and mail you potential hits, but there's a turnaround time and also . . ."

"It's fucking stupid?"

"Yeah, basically." She laughed. "Do you want some coffee?" I nodded and she added another scoop before sitting down at the table, far away from me. "Seems there are certain advantages to being over thirty. I remember how to print résumés and check newspapers."

I thought about Tobey and how résumé printing must be good for business.

"I mean, I might do Monster for the long term," she said. "You can ask them to put you on a tickler for certain companies or jobs and they'll buy all the papers and check them for you if something pops up, but I'm not waiting for that."

"Find anything?"

"Yeah. Google!"

"You found a job listing for Google in a newspaper?" I asked. I wanted to call it ironic, but spending my youth shaming Alanis Morissette had taught me that word was just too dangerous to use. "What does Google need with a pharmaceutical copywriter?"

"I'm not sure, but I'm applying. It's Google. They ride Segways and stuff. It's cool."

Picturing Romaya on a Segway made me happy. I could see her learning tricks down corporate hallways. It seemed to make her happy too, but she was careful not to see it too clearly. Wanting things was dangerous.

"Maybe I'll apply too," I joked, and she laughed.

"With your search history," she said, "not only wouldn't they hire you, they'd call the sex police."

"Good point. Maybe I'll call Bing. My porn history's immaculate there."

"You still on disability?" she asked.

I couldn't pretend that wasn't meant to shame me. "Yes. Free money," I said. "But there's more."

Now she was listening.

"I'm not sure if it made the news out here, but a couple

of months ago, did you catch stories about an 'Internet Messiah'?"

"What do you mean?"

"Some dude in New York they said would bring back the Net."

"Oh right. Yeah?"

"Well . . ."

I didn't finish the sentence, deciding instead to open my arms and let context make it easier.

"Well what?" she asked.

"Me. I'm the Internet Messiah."

"What does that even mean?" she asked.

"I just explained. I'm the guy who's bringing back the Net."

"You are?"

"No, I mean I'm the guy they say is going to do that."

"Yeah, well why do they say that?" she asked, and I wondered why I hadn't been expecting questions.

"It's hard to explain," I said, reaching into my backpack again, "but I have a copy of my journal. It's not long . . ."

Romaya went to get the coffee. "You want me to read your journal?"

"Well, it's more of a book. I dunno. I was in a bad way. I know that. I'm sorry. For a lot of things actually, but it might help explain. When the Net went down, I had nothing else to do. I started to sorta just look for it."

"Under rocks and stuff?"

"I know. It's weird," I said, and laid a copy of the journal down beside me. "But please don't make it harder. It wasn't much of an investigation, I admit, but here's the thing—that Jeeves guy? The psychic?"

She lit up a bit. "The dude who predicted O'Reilly's death?"

"Yes! Him. He swears I'm the one who will return the Internet. And there's this guy from 4Chan who's asking about me too."

"4Chan?"

"It's just a shitty Web site where terrible people do awful sometimes hilarious things, but it's also tied up with Anonymous sort of."

"You know this sounds insane, right?"

"Yeah, I know it's crazy that people could ever believe in me, but, y'know, they don't know I'm a fucking ass-hole, so I fooled someone, I guess."

"You can't talk to me like that anymore," she said. "Do you want your coffee or are you leaving?"

"Please read the journal," I said. "I think it will help you understand."

"That you're the Internet Messiah?"

"No. Just me. I think it will help you understand me."

"Why now?" she asked.

"Because I want you to come with me."

"What? Where?"

"I want you to help me look for the Internet. I mean California makes more sense anyway. Silicon Valley. Google. All that stuff."

"Wow, you've really studied up on this," she said. "Google and *all that stuff*. What do you even know about the Internet?"

"Well, not a lot at first, but I did actually read a bunch about it when . . . "

I reached out for the coffee she was holding so I could take a sip and reorganize my mind.

"Look," I said. "You've got a three-month severance. Come take an adventure with me. Tobey too. It'll be fun."

"You want me to drop out of my life and go on an adventure?"

"Not drop out. Seems your life already kicked you out."

"Right, and I'm going to fix that." She pointed to the classifieds as proof of her good intentions. Evidence that she did not deserve the fate of the unemployed.

"Great. Fix it. I'm not asking you to open a detective agency with me, but I'm going with this. Because I can. And now, for a little bit at least, you can too. And I'd like you to come with me because it's not about rent or getting pregnant or figuring out life. It's just an adventure. An honest-to-goodness, California, behind-the-scenes adventure. Why shouldn't you be there? We deserve an adventure."

Those were the wrong words. I should have steered clear of the miscarriages, but I stopped knowing the right words long ago—and besides, the wrong words had to be better than silence. I'd already tried that. Romaya came closer and picked up the journal, flipping through it dispassionately. Then she placed it alongside the classifieds.

"So. Where does this adventure take place?" she asked.

"What?"

"What's your plan? Your agenda? Shouldn't the messiah have a destination?"

"I don't know," I said. "It doesn't work like that. It's more intuitive. A feeling."

"You want me to give up on getting a new job to follow your feelings?"

"It's just a few weeks, months . . ."

"It's like you're still twenty-one, playing in some band and waiting to be 'discovered.' The world doesn't work like that. We have to make the effort."

"I didn't mean to upset you," I said, and put my coffee in the sink.

"I'm not upset. I just have to plan, and I think you should too."

"I never had trouble working when we were together," I said, zipping up my Jansport. "I hated it, but I did it. I only stopped when you left." I hung the bag off my right shoulder, just like I did in college, and walked over to Romaya. "There's a chance. A chance I'm not foolish."

"I know that. I know you can do lots of things if you want to."

I waited for more, but that was as much kindness as there'd be today. Maybe the book would bring more.

"Let me know what you think of the book," I said. "It's really for you anyway."

I'd written "for Romaya" on the first page, along with Tobey's address on the back so she'd know where I was staying, but she didn't respond. She just looked over at the journal resting on top of the classifieds.

"I have something else for you, too," I said, and upon saying it, realized it was all I had for her.

She waited instead of speaking.

"You don't have to frame it or cherish it," I said. "But it belongs with you. I gave it to you. Will you please take back the love letter I wrote?"

I took it out of my inside jacket pocket and unfolded it. Crinkled. Air-dried from the Hudson, but legible. Preserved.

"That looks like it's been through hell," she said.

"It has," I said. "Some things don't do well away from home." Too slick. Even true words can be wrong.

I could have dropped it there. Ran for the door with a no-backsies move, suitable for the child she thought I still was, but it would have been a hollow victory. I needed her to take it. To want it. But she didn't. I returned the letter to my pocket with as much quiet dignity as I could muster before leaving her apartment in silence. I would go on. I would get to where I was going. And it wasn't until I shut the door behind me and headed for the road that I remembered you can't hail a cab in this fucking city.

About three days later, it became very clear to me that Tobey was a good friend. It was pushing two weeks and he hadn't even begun to give me shit about crashing on his couch. He even let me copy his key. Maybe he was doing a slow burn or maybe I'd appeased him with several pizza purchases and kitchen cleans, but of all the things weighing on me, he was not one of them. And that night, it seemed my diminished spirits concerned him enough to come up with a plan.

"Gladstone," he said, offering me a tallboy from his fridge. "We've got to get you laid."

"Thanks Tobey," I said, "but you're not exactly Clive Owen, so I'll need more than a beer."

"You went with Clive Owen for that joke?" Tobey asked.

"Yeah, I'm getting old," I agreed. "I don't know who to be gay for anymore."

"Seriously. Let's hit a bar. It'll be good for you. Get you out of the house and into a Californian."

"That's not really my thing, Tobes. It's always too loud to talk. Getting judged on your cologne and clothes. I hate it."

"Oh, no. Not a *real* bar. Yeah, that would be awful. No I meant a sponsored bar."

Tobey explained that during the Apocalypse, dating sites had been raising revenue by throwing events at bars, where you paid an admission fee and filled out a questionnaire. Coordinators then interpreted the results and grouped like-minded individuals for some sort of vaguely entertaining twenty-first century dating game/auction. So around eight, we headed for Tobey's Matrix.

"Would it *kill* you to lose that fedora?" Tobey asked.

"I'm sorry, Tobes," I said. "I know your Black Flag T-shirt is the epitome of fashion, but I'm keeping the hat."

"*And* the white sports jacket?"

"Yes. Both. I'm in L.A."

"Why does a *Miami Vice* jacket mean *L.A.* to you?"

I stopped for a moment. "Hmm, that *is* curious. Anyway, I'm willing to take my chances."

Tobey drove us to a bar on some street I barely noticed because being aware of my surroundings was starting to make me uneasy. The bar looked standard and fratty, but there was a blue banner hanging outside that read, "OKCupid."

"Why are we going to an OKCupid bar?" I asked Tobey.

"Instead of? . . ."

"I dunno, Match.com? eHarmony?"

Tobey looked at me with vague disgust. "Gladstone, are you looking for someone to see a Coen Brothers movie with you or get your dick sucked?"

Inside, there were lots of seats, just like at the Hash Tag, and that was nice. Not sure why it took the Apocalypse to get some decent bar seating. Or maybe it was an L.A. thing. We paid our forty dollar entrance fee which came with two free-drink tickets, and a form of about twenty questions, replete with a tear-off number for identification.

"What did you put for the sexual-preference description?" Tobey asked.

" 'Somewhat adventurous.' How about you?"

"Sex criminal."

"That's not a choice," I said.

"I wrote it in," Tobey replied. "You think they grade these by Scantron?"

"Fair enough." I crossed out my answer and scribbled in "pervert."

When we were done, we handed our finished forms to one of the four perky young coordinators, two girls and two guys with lots of smiles. After about thirty minutes, some local comic emcee got up on a makeshift stage, not unlike the one at The Hash Tag.

"Jesus," I said. "When the Net went down, I should have invested everything into plywood."

"Yeah," Tobey agreed. "And desperation."

Apparently, they were trying to split the crowd up into four distinct personality types and make pairings. Having seen our coordinators, I was pretty sure the process was less than scientific. And when they called the numbers, I was even more sure, because Tobey and I were in the same group.

We took the stage, standing in a line with fifteen other guys, while the emcee started introducing us by reading our three-line bios. I seemed to be the oldest. (Indeed, that's why Tobey didn't even bother taking us to a Tinder bar). I could tell instantly that this was a highly flawed re-creation of a dating site, even if I'd never been on one. Nothing could be less like the Internet than consensually being put up on stage for harsh viewing.

"You're missing the point," Tobey said. "None of that matters."

"Doesn't it?" I asked. "Isn't that what the Net's about? Putting your best foot forward. Slimming pics. Lying about your height?"

"Yeah, a bit, but not dating sites so much. On a dating site the main point is you're on a dating site."

I didn't understand.

"Look," he continued. "You hit on a woman in a bar, a bookstore, a coffee shop, whatever, she can be annoyed with you. Maybe she's just trying to drink her skinny latte without being bothered. And even if she'd like to be hit on by a dude who's not you, she can still pretend she's not on the market. But on a dating site you're saying, yes, hi, I'm generally interested."

"That sounds kinda rapey, Tobes."

"I don't mean it like that. Of course, people get nixed on dating sites all the time, but just being there pulls back one more layer. Destroys the cool front. Everyone is admitting that, yeah, they'd like to meet someone. It levels the playing field a bit. It's more honest."

I was thinking about how the Net could catalyze honesty and deceit in equal measure when the emcee pulled a bit of a dick move on the first guy, who was wearing a short-sleeve button-down shirt and giving off a distinct IT vibe.

"According to your stats, here," he said, "you're five-foot-ten?"

The dude was my height at best, and I was glad I never lied about being five-foot-seven. He put his head down before saying weakly, "What? No. That's a mistake."

"Aww, it's okay," the emcee continued. "I'm just fucking with you." He flipped through the pages quickly. "Everyone lies about their height at these things."

"I didn't," I said.

"What was that?" the emcee asked.

"I didn't lie," I repeated.

He looked me up and down. "Are you sure? You look like someone who'd make himself bigger."

"Actually," I said, "I was hoping someone else would take care of that tonight."

The emcee paused for a second.

"He means his dick," Tobey clarified, and the audience lost it. A few women catcalled like they were at a bachelorette party.

I was in for it. As a comic it was his duty to be the funny one, so now he had to destroy me, even if it was his job to actually facilitate hookups.

"Good job making enemies, G-Stone," Tobey whispered. "How long did that take? Five seconds?"

"I don't like taking shit, Tobes."

"Nooo," he corrected. "You love *not* taking shit. It's not exactly the same."

The emcee flipped the sheets looking for mine. "Ah, is this you?" he asked. " 'Gladstone?' Just one name like Madonna or Cher?"

I didn't remember omitting my first name, but I wasn't sure it was a bad sign. Dr. Kreigsman had said using just "Gladstone," as I'd done online for years, was a way of being less than a complete person, but part of me also felt OKCupid didn't deserve all of me.

"Yes, that's me," I said, and I felt a strange energy pass through the crowd. I didn't know what it was, but my name had started something.

"Okay, Gladstone," he said. "Let's start with you. What brought you here tonight?"

"My friend Tobey."

That got a chuckle, but it rightly angered the comic as a petulant half-joke. He geared up to say something particularly pointed.

"Okay, okay," he said, "but what—"

"I came for the sex," I interrupted, hoping to diffuse his pending attack.

"Hey, that's a smooth line, buddy. Me Gladstone. Me come for bang bang."

"Well, I was hoping to have sex with a woman, not a primate, but yes. My name is Gladstone and I came here looking for a nice, attractive woman who would think I was worth having sex with."

I waited for a bucket of pig blood to fall on me all *Carrie*-esque, but it didn't. And that's when I realized this actually was like the Internet because honesty came easily. My time here was fleeting, and these people didn't know me. This was not my home. I had nothing to lose from the truth. And even though honesty wasn't hard, and there were countless other people in the room who could have been just as forthright, there was still something rare and startling about hearing the truth. And that was like the Net, too. Now I was bulletproof. Nothing could be done to me except by the worst of trolls. Trolls like the emcee. But I knew exactly where he was going.

"Well, let me ask you this, Mr. Honesty," he said. "How big—"

"Seven inches, cut."

He was done. He looked at the audience to make sure of what he already knew: they liked me and wouldn't like him if he were cruel. He was the kind of garbage who checked the consensus of a comment thread before leaving his opinion.

"I have a question," a woman in the audience said. She looked mid-twenties, wore a tight black T-shirt and jeans, and had one very fake streak of red through her otherwise brown and conservative hair. "Are you *the* Gladstone?"

"We're not up to the question section, ma'am," the emcee said, but she ignored him.

"Y'know, the Gladstone from that Internet Apocalypse book?"

I didn't understand what I was hearing. I looked at Tobey, and although he wasn't the picture of clarity, he seemed less thrown than I.

She called out to the bar. "Jimmy, can you grab my book, back there by the ice? The pages?"

The bartender looked beneath the counter and held up a stack of photocopied pages held together by a binder clip. "This?"

"Yep," she said, and then repeated her question to me in the form of a raised eyebrow.

"It's your book, dude!" Tobey said.

"Fuck, Tobey. How many copies did you make?"

"It's not all me. People started coming in to make copies for themselves the last couple of days."

"Um, this book," I said to the woman. "It's about a dude looking for the Net, and Oz and Romaya, and . . . "

"And Tobey," Tobey added.

"Yeah, because if it's you," she said, "I'm thinking I'd like to buy you a drink."

Something about this moment was even more surreal than being dubbed the Internet Messiah, but I knew it was real. This room had a smell. I was seeing it from behind my own eyes, and I had to embrace it.

"Well, then," I said, as painfully cool as I could muster, "why don't we get out of here?" I took a step off the stage.

"Can't. I'm a waitress," she said holding up her tray. "I don't get off for another two hours."

"Smooth, G-Stone," Tobey said as I stepped back on the stage.

"So you wrote a book?" the emcee asked, trying to regain control.

"Sort of. It's hard to explain."

"It's more like a journal," another dude said, and held up his copy, curled and contained by a rubber band.

"I have it too," another woman said, standing beside him and pulling out her copy.

"Tobey?" I asked. "What's going on?"

He was beaming. "Your book, dude," he said. "It's gone paper viral!"

The waitress' name was Wendy, and it was a good thing she wanted to take me home because Tobey took his

Matrix and went off with some woman wearing a hemp necklace and Snorg T-shirt.

"My roommates are out," she said, "so we'll be able to talk better in my apartment than in some noisy bar."

So this was a sure thing, it seemed, and I didn't know what to make of it. I'd been pedaling uphill for as long as I could remember. Now the road had leveled. Maybe there was even a decline that would let me coast all the way to a somewhat cluttered, even dirty, apartment on Kilkea Drive.

"Check it out," she said, revealing a bottle of Jameson as she returned from her kitchen.

"This is so weird," I said, from the couch. "You don't know me, but you know what I drink."

"Why is that weird?" she asked, taking a swig right from the bottle. Some dripped down her chin. "I read your book."

She caught the drop on her finger and straddled my lap. "What better way to get to know someone," she said, and ran the drop of Jameson over my lips and into my mouth. I tried to remember if she'd washed her hands after coming home from work, but hoped the alcohol would provide enough of a disinfectant.

"Besides," she said, taking her finger from my mouth. "It's not like I bring home the author of every book I read. I'm not a starfucker."

"I'm hardly a star," I said. "Just some broken mess with a journal full of crazy."

"Oh, I know," she laughed. "So why be so suspicious?"

She took off her shirt with a confidence I never saw in college. No bra and both nipples pierced. That was new. Of course, the right thing to do now was to have sex, but

I delayed. Maybe it was because I hadn't been with a woman in over two years. (Delusions don't count.) Or maybe it was because, having found someone who liked me, I really wanted to understand why.

I pulled back from the approaching kiss and said, "Yeah, but that's the thing. That guy in that book. He's just a bruise. Why would you like that?"

"Sometimes being broken is hot," she said, throwing my fedora to the side and pushing off my sports jacket.

"You wanna fix me?"

"I'm not sure I'd say fix." She ran her hands up my T-shirt. "But I'd like to make you feel better for a little while."

I decided not to press it any further and turned to my side, transitioning her flat to the couch without too much effort.

"Should we stop talking about the book?" I asked, and stroked the strands of red-dyed hair back from her face.

"Yeah, except I think it would be kinda hot to role-play it a bit," she said.

I pressed down on the couch, rising up high enough to look her straight in the eyes. "I don't know. I think pretending you were Romaya would really mess me up right now."

"Romaya?" she laughed. "No. I meant Oz."

"Oh, I guess that makes more sense."

"Yeah. Fuck me, Daddy," she said, quoting Oz from the journal, but she was trying too hard. It was wrong. Just not wrong enough for me to leave.

———

It turns out Wendy wasn't much of a snuggler, or so she said, but she was nice about getting me the number for a cab.

"Do you have a phone?" I asked, looking around her living room.

"Yeah," she said, "but they shut it off. It's hard to get used to mailing checks." She pointed to a stamped, unsent bill sitting on the table beside me.

"Okay, then," I said, pocketing the business card.

"There's a pay phone they got working on the corner at Melrose," she said, and sat up, tucking a blanket over her breasts and under her arms.

"Okay," I said, not knowing one-night-stand etiquette.

"Come here." She smiled and patted the couch beside her. "You forgot your hat."

I sat beside her and she placed the white fedora on my head before scratching at my scruff. That's when I realized something that made me laugh.

"What is it?" she asked.

"You're right. You didn't care about having sex with an author."

"Right," she agreed.

"You wanted to fuck the actual fictitious character."

She smiled and straightened the brim of my hat. "Well, my first thought would be to ask you why you'd call a diary 'fiction,' but yeah, I guess that's true."

I stared at her not knowing what to say.

"Besides," she said, "you're not that Gladstone."

"No?"

"Nah," she said. "You're softer."

"Oh."

"And stronger," she added, and grabbed me just below the shoulders, running her tight grip down my arms.

"Well, thank you for the vote of confidence." I kissed her forehead and headed for the door.

"Oh, and Gladstone," she said. "There's a mailbox by the pay phone. Do you think you could mail that envelope? Keep forgetting."

I headed to what I hoped was Melrose, taking comfort in the fact that for once I had every excuse to get lost. It turned out not to matter. Nearly the moment I hit the street, a parked car flipped on its headlights and crept closer. The limo pulled up beside me, and the back window rolled down to reveal a man in a black robe and a rubber clown mask like the one Heath Ledger wore during the bank heist in *The Dark Knight*.

"Need a ride?" he asked.

"Do I know you?"

"We're acquainted," he said. "Join me." His chauffeur, wearing a Guy Fawkes mask, exited the car and opened the door.

"Quiffmonster42?" I asked, and the clown nodded. I studied his mask and his robe. His stillness. "How do I know it's you?" I asked.

He raised a gloved hand to his brow and shook his head. "You're still not getting the whole Anonymous thing, huh?"

That sounded like something Quiff would say. I stepped inside and shut the door.

"Why'd you change your mask?" I asked, and he raised the partition separating the driver from us.

"Guy Fawkes is old hat, Gladstone," he whispered. "Just because there's no Net doesn't mean time stands still. It's not 2007."

"But—"

"I know, I know," he said, gesturing slightly to the driver. "Not everyone got the memo. So. Can I get you a drink?" He presented his 1970s-style limo wet bar. Quiff's regal manner seemed to match these surroundings far more than the Bowery Poetry Club where we'd met before.

"I'll pass," I said and he paused.

"Good for you, Gladstone. A little slap and tickle bring back the old confidence?"

I didn't like the question and I didn't answer.

"I apologize. That was coarse," he said, "and unimportant. What I really care about is your investigation."

I remembered the night we met. I stood on a chair and announced to 4Chan that I was looking for the Internet. It hurt to remember, because now he was one more person I'd have to disappoint. One more person to tell a story too long to explain. I stared at the hem of his robe and realized it was the first time I'd put my head down since I came to L.A.

"Quiff," I said. "I may have oversold myself."

"Chin up, Gladstone. I read all about it," he said, and patted yet another photocopy of my journal on the seat beside him.

"You read that?" I asked.

"Yeah. Quick question: Why did you spell my handle, 'Q-U-I-F-F?' Queef is spelled 'Q-U-E-E-F'"

"Pretty sure Urban Dictionary spells it Q-U-I-F-F."

"No, it does no such thing. The preferred spelling is

with the double "e." If you spell it with an 'i,' then it only takes one 'f.'"

"Oh," I said, forgiving myself for not double-checking the spelling during the Apocalypse. "I hope you weren't too offended by my misspelling your vagina-fart name. That must have been so embarrassing."

"I'll say," Quiff said, with a tiny laugh. "Especially because everyone's reading it. Really taking off."

"Tobey said it's going 'paper viral.'"

"The real Tobey?" Quiff asked.

"Yeah. The real one," The light caught the shine of the silkier material around his hem.

"Anyway, don't beat yourself up about the investigation too much," Quiff said. "After all, you've gotten this far. Anointed by Jeeves, a paper viral sensation, and . . ."

"And?"

"And you're in my car. Look around. Not just anyone rides with me."

"But none of that has anything to do with finding the Internet," I said. "You read the book. I wasn't looking for the Internet. I used the Net as a distraction when my life fell apart, and when it left, I made my investigation the new distraction."

I'd created silence with speech and I thought about the possibility of having proved a point, but Quiff took it away.

"Very eloquent. Did Dr. Kreigsman have you memorize all that?"

"You know about him?"

"We are Anonymous. We know things. The Internet was one way of finding and sharing information, but even without it, information exists. It can be acquired. We acquire it and we want to help you."

I wondered what kind of help could come from an angry clown.

"I have a present for you," Quiff said.

He picked up my journal to reveal a fairly thin book beneath it, about the size of a fashion magazine.

"Take a look," he said, handing it over. "Do you know what you're looking at?"

I flipped the pages. It looked a lot like a phone book.

"I think I read about this," I said.

"Shh. I'm going to tell you anyway," Quiff said, adjusting his mask and sitting up straight. "When the Internet began, they called it the ARPANET." He sounded like a children's librarian, explanatorily animated. "It was a U.S. project designed simply to link computers. To create networks. The ARPANET formed a connection between the military's defense researchers, either within the military itself or at ARPA-funded universities. Military and academia. They were the first to get online."

"Right. I read all about this in the hospital."

"Quiet," Quiff reprimanded. "By 1980, the number of people who had access to the ARPANET was growing. A few thousand now had e-mail addresses."

I got excited. "Right, so this is like the first Internet phone book," I said, interrupting again.

"Yes. It has names, e-mail addresses, phone numbers, and even postal addresses," Quiff confirmed.

I ran my hands over the cover. Still soft like a magazine, but of slightly heavier paper stock. Just enough effort to look more than completely forgettable. But it wasn't its appearance that made it special; it was its purpose. A phone book for the Internet, proving that people need to take the infinite and unknowable and quantify it in a form they can comprehend. It was like the Bible.

"So that's your first clue," he said.

I didn't understand. "What can I do with this?"

"This is where it starts."

"Yeah, but it grows into nothing," I insisted. "More and more people got online, ARPANET grew into the Internet, and this book grew to the point of absurdity until it ceased to exist."

"Incorrect."

"Incorrect?"

"Incorrect."

"What do you mean, incorrect?" I asked.

"Yes, the ARPANET continued to grow and moved into the private sector with the help of Senator Gore's bill."

I interrupted Quiff again. "I know. He *did* take the initiative in bringing the Net to the private sector. And that's all he ever said."

"The election's over, Gladstone, but, yeah, they really fucked him with that 'invented the Internet' bullshit. Anyway, more and more people got online, but the book did not grow."

Quiff pulled the flow of his black robe off the seat to his right, and there, on the dark leather was another phone book. He handed it to me.

"Take a look, Gladstone."

The new book was similar, but approximately 25 percent thinner.

"This is the phone book from 1988," he said.

"It's smaller," I said.

"Now he's getting it," Quiff said, knowing he had me. I listened even more intently to get him to continue, and, somehow, I could tell he was smiling behind the mask.

"But more and more people got online," I said. "Why would it shrink?"

"Well, fairer to say it changed. The book is still maintained, even now, but it no longer documents who's online. As you say, that's millions. Now it records the power brokers, the robber barons of the Net. Those who maintain real control."

I took the decanter of Scotch from the wet bar and poured myself two fingers, neat. Quiff made some sort of guttural sound from behind the mask.

"What? You offered," I said.

"No. Nothing. I was going to invite you to have some Glenlivet. Not sure what's in that old thing, but it's fine."

"Oh," I said. "Not picky," realizing I had no right to be an arbiter of fine taste in this company.

I took a sip and felt the sting of smoke far too strong to ignore. I almost coughed fire like a cartoon, but then it gave way to the comfort of moss and dirt. In another moment, I'd have the warm comfort of scorched earth.

"Fuck. Whatever that is, it's certainly something, Quiff."

"High praise indeed," he said.

"I don't know about this book stuff, though," I said.

"You don't have to know. We know. The book exists. Do you think the world's omnipotent would let the most important invention of the twenty-first century exist freely? Do you really think they wouldn't find a way to integrate themselves deeper and deeper into the process?"

"No, I can believe that," I said. "But why paper?"

"These are old soldiers, Gladstone. The most distrustful of the technology they helped make a reality. There is no trace of this online. E-data is forever, but paper burns."

I could see the deep black of Quiff's shoes even in the darkness of the limo. They stood out, polished with something deeper than shadows. He recrossed his legs and adjusted his robe.

"Let me simplify this for you. You don't have to tackle the whole World Wide Web. Find the latest book. If you do that, you limit our search for those few who had the power to take it away."

"I'm just some guy. Why don't you look for it?"

"You don't think we've looked for it?" he said, clearly annoyed. "You think Anonymous was sitting around waiting for some jackass from New York to save the day?" Quiff straightened his mask. "No offense."

"Well, no, I didn't think that. So, yeah, why me?"

"Look, we've tried, Gladstone. We're still trying, but it's time to put it in the hands of someone new. And besides, you have friends. Better than friends—fans. They'll *want* to help you. To join you."

"That sounds parasitic," I said.

"It's not parasitic. You're offering them a chance to be part of something. It's a lot better than sticking your Kickstarter account in someone's face. Or are you just afraid of a little hard work?"

I had told myself my contempt for returning to work was not laziness. That I simply could no longer get it up for labor that meant nothing. Now I was presented with something of significance. What possible reason for refusal could I give without simultaneously admitting that all I wanted was to do nothing?

"Can I count on you for assistance?" I asked.

"We will be there, Gladstone. Are you ready to gather the troops?"

I finished the rest of the Scotch in my crystal and waited for twenty-five smoky years of wooden gestation to settle and warm my resolve from the inside out.

"Troops? This is an investigation," I said. "I don't want war."

Quiff pulled back on the rubber of his mask until his eyes were firmly in line with the holes. "That doesn't matter, he said. "If you lead a good investigation, Gladstone," the war will want you."

Part II

5.

I sat completely still in the darkness of Tobey's apartment. Almost no one in the world knew where I was, and even those hip to my whereabouts couldn't find me here. Not if I didn't move. And in the comfortable quiet of invisibility I thought about becoming a new man. The one people were asking me to be.

"What do you make of this messiah business?" Dr. Kreigsman had asked, back at the hospital.

Back then, he had me convinced Jeeves never anointed me. That I'd heard the Internet Messiah story on the news, maybe even seen Jeeves in Central Park, but then just mentally assumed the identity of that mystery man in my memories. Still, I remembered the park. I could see Jeeves stammering and gesturing from my point of view and I knew, if I really thought about it, that it was true even then.

"What? You don't like it? Ask Jeeves," I said.

"How old are you, now?" Kreigsman asked.

"Thirty-seven."

"Have you achieved what you've wanted in life?"

Dr. Kreigsman had to know that was a betrayal I couldn't forgive.

"You know I haven't," I said. "You don't have to be cruel."

He took off his glasses.

"Well, let's talk about that," he said, polishing the lenses. "Why is it cruel? Why is it cruel for you to be just another man?"

I hesitated.

"Don't worry about sounding arrogant," he said. "I won't judge you."

"Because," I said, still embarrassed, "I think I'm smart."

"I think so too. Exceptionally so." Kreigsman put his glasses back on and focused on me. "You'd have to be to write multiple identities in real time. And there's more."

I waited for the more.

"You're not a kid anymore. You're smarter than ever. Even an average man will start to have it all figured out by the time they're pushing forty. Except, for most, the trajectory of their lives is already set by the time they acquire that kind of wisdom."

"I don't understand where you're going with this," I said. "Also, you missed a spot on your right lens."

He took his glasses off and dropped them in the chest pocket of his lab coat.

"When you're talented and unrecognized, that starts to feel a lot like persecution. And if you're particularly talented—well, that might start to feel like persecution on a biblical level."

I didn't say anything. Kreigsman came closer and placed his hands on my shoulders. "You're a very bright guy," he said. "But you don't need to be the Messiah."

Just then Tobey opened his door and slapped on the lights in one drunken motion. "Holy shit," he said, finding me instantly revealed in the fluorescent glow. "You have *got* to be the Messiah."

"Why?"

"That girl practically devoured me. She had a friend too. And all because I'm in your book. This shit is blowing up."

"Mazel tov, Tobes. You've really made a compelling case for me assuming the mantle of savior against unknown agents of the Apocalypse."

"Did I mention there was butt stuff?" he said.

I flipped Tobey the phone book Quiff had given me.

"What's this?" he asked.

"A clue."

I explained to Tobey everything there was to know about the Internet phone book. About how Quiff had given us a starting place a way to find who stole the Internet by understanding who *could* steal it. He did an excellent job of feigning interest while presumably fantasizing about cruising the West Coast and tagging groupies who would continue to spread his legend. We agreed we would be a team. We would take that New York panic attack masquerading as an investigation and make it real on the West Coast. We would assume a job title we didn't understand. Not systems analyst or subrogation claims manager, but Internet Messiah. And assistant.

"Assistant?" Tobey asked.

"You'd prefer disciple?"

"Fuck that," Tobey said. "I want to be co-Messiah."

"Yeah, sorry, I'm the anointed one, but since all you care about is getting laid, may I offer that you don't need to be the Messiah? You don't have to be the lead singer. The drummer gets all the chicks."

"Good point," Tobey agreed. "I'll just be the Tobey."

"There you go."

"So I don't work Wednesdays. We can start this shit tomorrow?"

"Tomorrow's Tuesday?"

"Yeah, I know, I'll call in sick so I can have a two-day midweek weekend, duh."

We would have slept 'til noon, but the 7:45 knocking wouldn't allow it, and I opened Tobey's door more concerned with removing one half of the percussion equation than seeing who was on the other side. It was Romaya. Her hair was tied back, and she was wearing a blouse and business suit, but something was wrong. She had been crying, or almost crying. She had that tiny shake in her voice.

"What's the matter?" I asked.

"I have an interview at Google at two o'clock today."

"Wow, that's great, Babe. Congrats."

"No it's not," she said. "Google's in Palo Alto, five, six hours away."

"Oh . . . so?"

"Do you think you could drive me?"

"Drive your car?"

"No. My car's out of commission. Does Tobey have a car? He must, right? Everyone has a car here."

"Yeah, but . . ."

Romaya looked over my shoulder in vague alarm, but

before I could turn around I heard, "Yes, you can borrow my car, strange MILF-y lady." Tobey was wearing a T-shirt and boxers.

"She's not a MILF," I said. "She's my wife. My ex-wife." I took a breath and held up one finger. Then I started again. "Tobey, this is Romaya."

"Oh, shit," Tobey said. "Hi."

"Romaya," I said, "Tobey."

"Nice to meet you," she said, but her eyes lost focus before finishing. She was remembering her disdain for Tobey and what she thought was his frat fuck site. She never believed there was more to him, which bothered me, considering I had shared her dislike for frat fucks. My belief should have counted for something.

"Where we going?" Tobey asked.

"Google," I said.

"Oh, cool. Romaya's joining our investigation?"

"No. She has an interview."

"What investigation?" Romaya asked.

"The one I asked you to join," I said. "All the stuff in the book."

Romaya looked stuck and incomplete, like an accidentally saved e-mail that sits in your drafts until deleted.

"You didn't read my book?" I asked.

"Not yet, but we really have to go."

We hit the road pretty quickly and agreed Tobey, as the lifelong West Coaster, should drive. I'd be a menace, and Romaya wanted to review her résumé, portfolio, and library photocopies about Google. I offered her shotgun so she didn't feel like luggage, and took the backseat.

"So," Tobey said, turning to Romaya after entering the

5. "We're happy to take this little trip and all, but I'm a little confused about something."

Romaya put down her papers with too much effort.

"Google's like a big deal. If you got an interview, I'm surprised they didn't just fly you out."

That was a good point. And if I had any doubt about my sanity or Tobey being real, that clinched it, because there's no way in hell I would ever be practical enough to have such a thought on my own.

"Yeah, except I lied," Romaya said. "I told them I lived in Palo Alto to be a more attractive candidate. Y'know, so they wouldn't have to worry about me moving."

"Smart," Tobey said. He drove with his knees while he adjusted the radio and fixed his baseball cap.

"Yeah, well, that's why I'm screwed. Because they thought I was so close, they called me at the end of the day yesterday, thinking I could just pop in today for the two p.m. cancellation."

"You didn't have to take it," I said, but that was wrong, and Romaya didn't answer. Not taking it would mean accepting failure. I shook it up. "So what's wrong with your car?"

"Flat tire."

"On the way?" Tobey asked.

"No, I saw it when I went to leave this morning. I thought it looked low last week, but I didn't check because I've been biking everywhere."

Romaya was thinner than I noticed before. Not thinner, but harder.

"So yeah, I checked it out and there was a huge shard of glass in the tire."

"The wedding photo," I said.

"Yeah."

"Should have had the picture laminated."

Tobey didn't understand, but he knew enough to know he didn't have to understand everything. He let us talk. Except we didn't talk. Romaya returned to her lapful of information.

"So you couldn't change the tire?" he asked.

"I can change a tire," Romaya said, taking offense, "but I'm not going to drive three hundred miles on a donut, blow out again, and have to call Google to tell them I have a flat tire and I'm a liar who doesn't actually live in Palo Alto."

"Fair enough."

We left the Valley, and the road stretched out into nothing, although that was the wrong word, because our journey contained none of the tension or release of a stretch. It just was. California is straight and barren. It lets you drive with your knees. And even though we started to pass some orchards, it seemed to me nothing was supposed to live here. That the planet had other plans for this stretch of land besides humans.

"Wait a second," I said, breaking the silence. "Why didn't you rent a car?"

"Look, I'm sorry if I'm putting you out," Romaya said. "I wouldn't have asked if it weren't important."

"Not at all," Tobey offered.

"It's not that," I said, staring at the faux pearls my mother had bought her. "We were just wondering."

She closed her folder of papers. "For the same reason I didn't buy a new tire. Garages and rental car places don't even open until nine, and by the time I'd get out of there, I'd be late."

It made sense, but the weather changed by the time she finished her sentence. The sky grew dark and heavy, like we'd entered something more than a new zip code. Drops hit the window. Thicker than normal rain. Heavier. And when it landed, it radiated across the glass. Tobey's wipers sucked, spreading the remains, and producing a window more translucent than transparent. And that was a problem, because light was in short supply.

I thought about the time Romaya and I had done a New England vacation planned around a friend's Cape Cod wedding. We'd camped in Maine and then stayed at a Vermont bed and breakfast before hitting our destination. There are no streetlights in Vermont. Not where we were. And if you're driving east to west, there are sometimes no roads either. But what did that matter to two young people without children or an overbearing knowledge of mortality? We were a team. We were in a rented Nissan Altima and nothing could break the seal of our power-windowed love. That's how lovers think when they're young and stupid. Maybe that's just love. I don't know yet.

We took a Vermont drive into a darkness we'd never seen. And it wasn't just the lack of streetlights. It was the lack of anything. There was none of New York City's electric-light glow irradiating the night with a color less than pitch black. There was nothing but farms, and the darkness was so dark it looked wet. And the quiet was so quiet you knew you were pure. For now, you were in the control group of your life and all the things that would happen to you outside of this were the influences being tested. What would break you, strengthen you? What would make you the person you'd become? And

how would that person be different if you had just
stayed here in the quiet darkness with the person you
loved?

We pulled over to the side of the road and tried to stare
into the night, feeling like our eyes were closed even wide
open. It was one of the most beautiful and terrifying experiences of my life. And then it was broken. Rain hit
the glass and the night gave way to flashes of lightning.
Romaya wanted to stay, but for some reason I knew we
had to go. I pulled back out into the road and headed
straight, hands tight on the ten and two, and every time
the lightning flashed we saw the world I'd had the audacity to travel in blindness. There were trees. There were
wooden fence posts. There were grassy hills unknown to
us, and as we reached the very top, a giant rush of lightning illuminated a cloud formation we saw for only an
instant. And even though it was fleeting and impossible,
Romaya and I both swore we saw the face of God.

But there is no god on highway 5, and there's no devil
either, because there's not enough trouble to get into on
that patch of straight nothing. The wind picked up and
when we hit certain bumps it actually felt like the car
could get carried away. Romaya shut the radio off.

"What'd you do that for?" Tobey asked, the rain drill-
ing his windshield.

"Because it's getting scary out here. You need to concentrate."

"And someone told you I can't concentrate when *Firth
of Fifth* is playing?" He flipped the CD player back on,
accelerating slightly.

"Easy, Tobes," I said, but I was actually getting less
worried because the increased rain had washed his

window clean, overcompensating for his smudging, shitty wipers. We could see.

"One more question," Tobey said, keeping his eyes on the road. "Why'd you come to Gladstone? You didn't have any friends or closer neighbors you could ask?"

"It was seven fifteen when I realized I had a flat," Romaya said. "All my friends have jobs."

It was hard to know if that reproach was meant for Tobey or me, but it made a silence that lasted until the weather broke. Then the sun shined and the entire state of California went back to being a place where weather dictated happiness and happiness dictated the preservation of happiness.

"Do you like it here?" I asked Romaya.

"You know I do," she said.

"Well, no. I know you liked Eureka where you were born, but this is hardly that."

"Yeah, well, this is as close as I could get to home without being a lumberjack. I like it, but in many ways, it's not so different from New York."

"Seems to me," I said, "the major difference between New York and L.A. is that when you fail in L.A., you still get to live somewhere with a barbecue."

Romaya didn't laugh, but she nodded slowly. "That's really funny," she said with a slight sense of wonder. "You're still really funny."

I smiled. Tobey was at the wheel and the newfound California sunshine was making things right, like the most insistent of Instagram filters. We pulled up to the parking lot, and went through a gate where Romaya was expected.

As we pulled into a spot, Romaya said, "So I guess you

guys can like drive around Palo Alto for a couple of hours and then wait for me in the parking lot? Would that be okay?"

"Fuck that," Tobey said, jumping out of the car and closing the door.

Romaya fumbled for her handle. "Excuse me?" she said, stepping out and standing between the open door and car frame. Tobey spoke across the roof.

"We're going in. Or did you think the Internet Messiah and Tobey were gonna pass up an opportunity to get up close and personal with Google?"

"Seriously?" Romaya asked, now looking at me beside her.

"It's no joke," I said. "I know you didn't read the book, but others have. Lots of people now. It's taking off."

"I know," she said. "Even the fucking barista at Starbucks had it splayed open with a binder clip yesterday as she made my skinny latte."

"Yeah, well, we're on the job. It's not like I didn't ask you to be part of this."

"Part of what? You guys can't mess up my Google interview. I'm out of work. Do you not get that this is a big deal for me?"

Just then a criminally happy young woman called to us from curbside. She was standing on a Segway. "Hello! Ms. Petralia?" she asked. Maiden name. Romaya kept her back to the curb for a second to retrieve a new expression. Then she turned, all smiles.

"Yes, hello," she said. "Just getting my things."

She took a step from the car to pull down on her skirt, and I grabbed her folder of materials from the front seat.

I stood between her and Suzie Segway so she could gather herself as she adjusted her blouse.

"Hey," I said, and put my finger gently under her chin, like I did on our first date. She looked up slowly. "I promise we'll behave, Babe," I whispered. "And you'll do great. You got this."

She looked at me, and I nodded, forcing as much confidence into a smile as I could manage. Then I offered her the folder, but she was distracted by Tobey.

"No one's gonna mess anything up for you," he said, trying to echo my sentiment. "Besides, we have no choice. I doubt they'd let us back into the lot without you."

And as Romaya stared at Tobey and tried to divine his intent, I did a terrible thing. I took the love letter from my pocket and slipped it into her folder. Not terrible because it would fuck her up during the interview—there was no chance of that. I buried it deep in the very back of her papers. But terrible because it was cheating. A desperate attempt to get it home, based only on the hope that she'd realize it was a good thing once she noticed it living where it belonged.

"Look, just stick to the truth," Tobey said. "Say you had car trouble this morning and asked some friends for a ride. Just don't tell them we drove hundreds of miles. Trust me. That is an excellent lie."

And despite my best efforts, I had to admit that Tobey's scheming brought her more comfort than my support.

"Okay, but please behave," Romaya said. Then she took the folder from me and we closed up the car.

"Could you lose the hat?" Romaya asked me. "You look like a vacationing dentist."

I laughed and said, "Good. Jokes are good. They'll like

you more if you look like you're too happy to care about Google."

Suzie led us into Google headquarters and I couldn't help humming *World of Imagination* to myself from *Willy Wonka* as we were greeted by the high ceilings of red and yellow and blue. We got our superspecial Google badges, which we affixed to our T-shirts with a red plastic clip, and then we headed into a larger room. Suzie scooted ahead and did a quick U-turn. She opened her arms and said, "Would you care for anything to eat? We have everything."

I hadn't realized we were in an employee kitchen— probably because it was the size of half a football field. There were five or so glass-doored, industrial-sized refrigerators filled with juices, yogurt, and prepared sushi. All the counters had rows of drawers stuffed with Sun Chips and all manner of organic snackery. It was like being in a supermarket for insufferable twats, and I looked around for a cashier. There was none. My hesitation was visible.

"Yes, anything you want," Suzie said for my benefit.

Tobey didn't need further prodding. He was already opening and closing the pantry drawers with wild abandon. I wasn't really in the mood for prepackaged sushi, but how do you turn down free Google sushi? I thought about calling it "Gooshi" as I pulled a pack from the fridge, but I'd promised Romaya I'd be as boring as possible. She was also playing it safe, opting only for a bottled water. Tobey, however, kept pulling the drawers until Suzie spun around.

"Can I help you find something?" she asked. "We have fruit, yogurt, sushi, even some organic turkey jerky. Y'know, practically everything."

Tobey stopped on a dime. "Ah there it is," he said with a slight grin, freezing the drawer at half pull. "*Practically* everything. That explains why I can't find any Funyuns."

Suzie shrugged apologetically.

"Don't mind my friend," I said. "He still uses Yahoo because it has all his porn bookmarks."

"Okay . . . " Romaya said. "Maybe we should get me to my interview and let my companions continue this discussion without us."

"Oh, I don't mind," Suzie said, looking at me. "Also, Google Chrome can import all your bookmarks from your previous search engine. Once the Internet comes back that is."

"Thank you," I said. "Make a note, Tobey."

Suzie smiled and leaned into her Segway, a hair short of movement. "Well, now that you have snacks, let's get you situated so I can get Ms. Petralia to her meetings."

We followed Suzie down a corridor past a room of cubicles separated by some sort of appealingly obnoxious grass planters until we reached a room more suited to my interests: foosball tables, darts, old-time video games, new-time video games, and, just because they could, a giant kids' ball pit filled with Google-colored balls. The room was sparsely populated with employees so relaxed in their workplace environment that even I, out of work for two years on psychiatric disability, wanted to slap them for being damn millennial slackers.

Suzie raised her arms to the red, blue, green, and yellow ductwork and announced, "Have at it, boys." By the time she completed her phrase, there was only one boy. Tobey had run headfirst into the ball pit.

Suzie giggled in nervous surprise.

"Yahoo, am I right?" I said with a shrug.

Romaya was almost too annoyed to turn her nervous quiver into a smile for Suzie, but she managed. I straightened myself up like a professional and warmly offered my hand. "Thank you for your hospitality," I said. "Please don't let us keep you."

"Not at all," Suzie said. "Ready to go, Ms. Petralia?"

"Sure am."

I tried to wish Romaya good luck, but she was already following Suzie down the hallway to a future, unaware that my letter was tagging along.

"Gladstone!" Tobey called, bursting from the pit. "Get in here."

I put my sushi down on a ledge and walked over. "Y'know, you did promise Romaya you'd behave, jackass."

"I'm behaving. Get in here. *I have to talk to you . . .* " he whispered.

I stepped into the pit as gracefully as I could, which was not at all.

"I wanted to get off the camera," Tobey said, his head only slightly emerged from the colored balls.

"Why? We're not doing anything wrong," I said.

"Not yet. But are you seriously telling me the Internet Messiah and Tobey are going to go to Google and not investigate the Apocalypse?"

"Aside from promising Romaya we'd behave, what do you think we could possibly get away with before security booted us?"

"Why do you think I'm in the ball pit?" Tobey asked.

"Because you're functionally retarded?"

"Boo," Tobey said with only half his face emerging. "That's a fratty joke."

"No, a fratty joke would be because you like having balls on your chin."

"Homophobic."

"No, it's not. It's making fun of a frat boy's homophobia. Jesus, now even you don't get how satire works?"

"I know, jackass," Tobey said. "I'm satirizing people who don't understand satire."

Just then, a disproportionately loud CNN news banner graphic reading, "Internet Apocalypse" blasted across the huge TVs before dissolving into an insanely handsome anchor sitting beside my old friend Senator Melissa Bramson. Dr. Kreigsman had confirmed my memories of her and Christians Against the Messiah as true, but believed their protest pertained to some other e-messiah. It was disconcerting to see her from a sober point of view. And from a ball pit. That was weird too.

"Yesterday, standing beside the Liberty Bell, Pennsylvania's junior senator and founder of Christians Against the Messiah, Melissa Bramson, held a rally of more than two thousand supporters," the anchor read. "There, she lobbed criticisms at the Obama White House for not finding the so-called Internet Messiah, and she joins us in our studio now. Senator Bramson, welcome."

Bramson sat stiffly in a red blazer straight out of the Nancy Reagan collection. "Nice to see you again, Chris."

"Senator, we haven't heard anything about the Internet Messiah for a couple of months, and, frankly, it wasn't the largest story in the first place. Why all the fuss?"

"Well, because he's building an army." She dropped a copy of what I assumed was my journal on the counter.

"Ooh, nice velo binding," Tobey said. "Really classes it up."

"That, I take it," Chris said, "is the Internet Messiah's purported journal that's been spread around in the last couple of weeks?"

"It is, indeed. And if you thumb your way through this filthy manifesto, you'll see it is very clearly the message of someone leading a revolution."

"Huh," Tobey said. "And here I thought your journal had too much whacking off to be a proper manifesto."

The anchor said pretty much the same thing in gentler prose. "And what is that message, Senator? Because I have to tell you, I did read it, and I didn't see much in the way of politics. Some call it a love story."

Senator Bramson snorted, and I wondered if the surgeon who had built her nose anticipated such duress to the nasal cavity.

"Did you read it, Senator?" he followed up, showing an unusual amount of backbone for an anchor.

"Enough of it," she said. "You don't need to actually go down in the sewer to know it stinks. But the real question, Chris, is why has this administration done nothing to find him? This administration that can kill by drone strike, that can suspend constitutional rights under the NET Recovery Act, can't locate one smut peddler?"

"Didn't you sign the NET Recovery Act despite public outcry against its constitutional abuses?"

"Sure did. And if it wasn't to round up filth like this, then what was the point?"

"But round him up for what, Senator Bramson?"

"I don't know, Chris. That's the point. We haven't questioned him. Don't blame me for not being able to answer your questions when this administration's fallen asleep at that the wheel."

Just then the channel switched over to the Game Show Network. Some neck-bearded hipster without an appropriate amount of self-awareness and self-hatred had changed the channel from the comfort of his massaging reclining chair.

"Aww, too bad," Tobey whispered to me. "I'm sure she was just about to warm up to you too." Then he called out to the guy in the chair. "Buddy, any chance you could put that channel back for a minute?"

Captain Indifference turned to us, lowering his head and looking over the top of his plastic-framed glasses. "If it's important to you. . . ." he said.

I turned to Tobey. "And you call *me* a hipster douchebag."

The anchor had finished with Bramson, and he turned to the camera again.

"Joining us now with a further perspective on the so-called Internet Messiah is Special Agent Aaron Rowsdower of the NET Recovery Act's Special Task Force."

"Wait. Is that *the* Rowsdower?" Tobey asked.

The man on the screen was in his mid-forties, too thin, and too serious, but I wasn't sure it was the Rowsdower I remembered. Still, how many could there be?

"So Special Agent Rowsdower," Chris continued. "You've heard the Senator. What do you say to the allegations that this administration has fallen asleep at the wheel regarding the Internet Messiah investigation?"

"Well, first of all, I'm not here to give sound bites on behalf of this administration. I can speak only to the task force efforts to investigate the disappearance of the Internet, including our inquiries regarding so-called Internet Messiahs."

"Messiahs?"

"Yes. It puzzles me that Senator Bramson seems to think that only one person can proclaim themselves a messiah. Certainly the notion of multiple false prophets can't be unfamiliar to someone in politics."

"With all due respect," Senator Bramson said, "that's a dodge. I'm not interested in every crackpot. *This* so-called messiah has written a book. That's the one we're talking about."

"No, that's the one *you're* talking about, Senator, for some reason I can't understand. I've met this person you're referring to, and trust me: if he or any other person is behind the disappearance of the Internet or holds keys to its retrieval, we'll see him again."

"What can you tell us about this man?" Chris asked.

"Well, nothing. Speaking would be grossly irresponsible. But, y'know, do you need me to tell you anything? I mean, I know the senator isn't interested in reading the book despite her allegations, but it's all right there."

"Does that mean you endorse the book?"

"Endorse it? Who am I? To me, it's evidence. To the senator it's a basis for loose talk. I don't know what it means to you, Chris, but seems to me if someone hands you a diary, it's silly to ask questions about who they are."

The segment closed out and the Google recliner guy changed the channel. It was a commercial for the new iPhone, dubbed the iPhone Infinity—the first smart phone release of the Apocalypse. A woman's elegant hand handled it against an all-white backdrop. It looked just like the last iPhone, but with the sideways "8" infinity symbol in the Apple icon. The dude brought his recliner forward, taking an interest.

"No one knows when the Internet's coming back," a woman's voice said, "but when it does, won't you want the most powerful iPhone ever made?"

"So smart!" recliner guy said. "So fucking smart!"

I stepped out of the ball pit. "You think people will buy something that doesn't yet work?" I asked.

"Sure," he said. "And better yet, there'll be no shitty tech blogger dumping all over it the next day."

"And I guess," I said, "Mac fanboys can proclaim it as the best, fastest, most powerful phone and there'd be no way to prove they were wrong until the Net came back."

"Yep," he replied. "And that's when they'd introduce a new phone anyway."

"The Infinity Plus One," Tobey added, and the recliner dude laughed.

"Yeah, marketing in the Apocalypse is a whole new world," he said.

Tobey emerged from the ball pit. "Yeah," he said. "Whatcha working on?"

Chair dude made a face indicating such a question was clearly off-limits, or maybe he was just remembering that time he had a nonmicrobrewed beer. Either way, he said, "Come on. This is Google. We're not all ball pits and Segways."

"Sorry, it's just that our friend is interviewing here," I said. "She's a pharmaceutical copywriter so we were just curious."

"Well, sorry, I'm in analytics. . . ."

"Oh, is that why you're so not busy?" Tobey asked.

"I'm plenty busy," he replied, cranking up the vibration on his chair. "But you don't expect me to craft Apocalypsebusting code without my three o'clock vibrating massage, do you?"

The five-hour drive home felt like three. Maybe it's because the road's always shorter when you know the way, but probably because Romaya was happy. There was an energy from the moment Suzie returned her to us, but she didn't say a word until we were all back in the car.

"That went great," she said, mixing the hopeful prayers of the recently unemployed with a fourth-grade girl getting a gold star. "I think they liked me."

"I'm sure they did," I said. "That's great."

Tobey was all business. "Did they say why they're hiring in an Apocalypse?"

"Not really. One guy talked about setting up, like, Google stores where you could go online with other Google stores. Like a Google network connected to itself."

"Can you do that?" Tobey asked.

"Yeah," I said. "I mean, that's no different than everyone in the same office or offices being linked on one network, right? See, if they think that's feasible, that tells me the problem is only at the hubs—the points where all the individual networks are attached to each other."

"So Google's gonna make its own mini-network?" Tobey asked.

"I dunno," Romaya said, turning around to face me. "Only one dude said that, and offhandedly. It wasn't about their plans. It was about me. I talked about myself for three hours. You should do an interview there. You'd love it."

"Let's try this another way," Tobey said. "What was it about you they were so interested in?"

Romaya turned around to face front. "Mostly the copy I wrote for drugs that had gone generic."

Tobey didn't understand.

"After a while, drugs lose their patent and other companies can make generic versions," she explained. "Cheaper versions. Like how you can buy ibuprofen, but some people still pay more for Advil, right?"

"Who does *that*?"

"Lots of people. You still see Advil in stores. And Pfizer still runs ads for it—something generic manufacturers can't afford to do."

"So they were interested in your ads where you sell the more expensive version of things. . . ." I said, feeling that must be important.

"Yeah. So how did your investigation go?" Romaya asked, turning to face me again.

"Not so great. Still working with the Internet phone book as our main lead."

"What's that?"

I began to reply, but Tobey cut me off.

"I'm sorry, Romaya," Tobey said, "but we simply can't divulge that information until we know you're part of our team. Whaddya say?"

"I'm not part of your team," she replied.

"Oh, well then I'm sorry, but—"

This time I cut Tobey off. "It's a list of names of the power brokers of the Internet. Those with the most control. We're looking for the latest edition because Anonymous tells us each edition gets smaller, so it decreases our number of suspects."

"Anonymous told you?" she asked.

"Yeah."

"Wow."

I tried to be proud, but I knew that "wow" was merely acknowledging the approval of others.

"Well, don't be too impressed," I continued. "We have nothing exciting to report. Turns out I might not actually be the Messiah."

"Well, not that kind, right?"

"What kind?"

"The James Bond kind. Gathering data, going on missions. That's not your thing, is it?"

"I don't know. What's my thing?"

"I don't know. Ask your groupies."

"Please, Romaya. We call them disciples," Tobey corrected.

"Ask them what?" I pressed. "What my thing is? What kind of Messiah I'm supposed to be?"

"No, I meant you're an idea man. Ask them to do the James Bond stuff for you."

6.

The biggest difference between the real Tobey and the one in my journal was that the real Tobey believed in things. His failure to deliberate wasn't so much a sign of apathy as much as evidence that he simply wasn't plagued by doubt. But even if he didn't sweat the small stuff, he had a core. A belief system. And aside from the mere prospect of getting laid assisted by his pseudo celebrity, he truly believed in the Internet Messiah. That's not the same as saying he believed in me. More like he thought the Messiah was important, and he was happy to know the guy anointed to play him. So the next morning, he pushed for us to effectuate Romaya's plan: getting the disciples to do the James Bond stuff for us by sending them out to spy at Google, Facebook, or any Silicon Valley destination we could think of.

"We should hold a meeting at The Hash Tag," he said,

sparking his bowl of shwag. (He was motivated, but not to the exclusion of weed.)

"Okay," I said. "What did you think of Romaya?"

"She's a very nice lady," he said. "So I'll reach out to Jynx and set it up? Get you in front of your people?"

"Do you need your car today?" I asked.

"Not especially."

"I want to see Romaya. Maybe take her to that cemetery movie theater place you went to."

"Hollywood Forever? Yeah, you're in luck, they're doing movies every night now, but, um . . ."

"What?"

"You realize she's your *ex*-wife, dude," Tobey said.

"Yeah, but she's why I came out here."

"Sure, but keep in mind you're just about to get a tremendous amount of Internet Apocalypse tail."

You had to know Tobey. He said things like that knowing they sounded shallow and hedonistic, but his words had a distinct level of sarcasm. Not to say he didn't think this was a golden opportunity for sex. He did. And not to say he didn't fully intend to welcome that sex with open arms, but he knew it sounded fratty. His deliberately coarse speech was really more of an admission, even a confession, than some bro's bragging pep talk. And I liked him for it because almost every man I've ever met has run to the offer of easy sex, but most make a big show of being above it. They talk about misogyny and keep their sex egalitarian and polite. They shake their heads at the sexually brazen. And most of them are scared liars who will one day corner their platonic girlfriends with uncomfortable jokes and guilt trips, trying to up the ante into a sexual relationship with something that started merely as safe and respectful. Most will turn angry, spouting "friend-zoned" attacks while whining about the dangers of being a "nice guy." But Tobey was a nice guy. Every woman was safe and his dirty talk merely held up a sign of who he was for anyone interested in knowing more.

And while I respected all of that, it didn't change why I couldn't heed his advice.

"Yeah, I get it, Tobey," I said. "But I love Romaya."

While my sights were still set on a night with Romaya, we did spend all day focused on finding the Net.

"Let's put that phone book to work for us," he said as we drove through the area I'd come to know as Brentwood. "Give me some names from the book."

"But they're just names," I said, flipping pages. "Andreas Gibian of Dallas. Know him?"

"Nope."

"How about Claudette Dubois of Paris?"

"Maybe," Tobey said. "Does it say anything about her changing her name to Megan and tending bar at The Dirty Saddle on the Sunset Strip?"

"Sadly, the book is silent on that issue," I replied.

"Well, we'll just mark it down as a 'maybe' then," he said, and we drove on. The book was in alphabetical order, with names from all over the world. It was hard to pick out somebody good only a day-drive away. But then I had an idea.

I flipped to the Ls and then spoke with great confidence. "Drive to Westwood Village."

"Who's there?" Tobey asked.

"Professor Kevin Leonards, the UCLA professor who helped develop the Internet."

"Hey, I thought Al Gore inv—"

"Don't say it, Tobey."

"Aww, I'm just fucking with you. So why this guy?"

"Well, I learned about Leonards during my research at the hospital. I already knew about him. So I used his name to reverse engineer my search—basically, starting with the individual and then cross-referencing his name with the other listings in the Internet phone book."

"Don't you mean, you used the phone book just to look up the address of some dude you already read about?"

"Basically." I laughed. "But, y'know, father of the Internet. What more to do you want?"

"Works for me."

"Good," I replied. "We need to get to Thayer Avenue. Got a map?"

"Sure. Check the glove compartment. It's probably next to my axle grease and buggy whip."

We headed to Westwood, which reminded me a lot of where the kids went trick-or-treating in *E.T.* Maybe it was. That was exactly the kind of worthless thing I'd Google if I still could.

There was a long line of college kids running down the entire block preceding an Apple store. They were waiting for the iPhone Infinity.

"Neat," Tobey said. "Hey, maybe we can ask these fuckwads where Thayer is."

One of the kids had already secured his phone and was showing it off to his friends, who took turns holding it. "Oh man, this is gonna be awesome," one of them said.

"Yeah, I hope the Internet comes back right now just

so I can taunt you for the next hour until you get yours," the proud owner replied.

I looked at Tobey. "Hard to believe there are bigger assholes in this world than you," I said.

"It's a little breathtaking," he agreed. "Hey, guys," he called out. "Any of you know where Thayer Avenue is?"

Consensus placed it at about ten blocks away and we took their word for it, but not before one of the kids said, "More like Gayer Avenue, am I right?"

"You think they were being faux-homophobic?" I asked Tobey as we drove away.

"Probably," he said. "Unless they were talking about your hat."

There was no reason to believe Professor Leonards was alive, still at this address, or willing to talk to us, but no one could say we weren't trying, and we felt our chances were best showing up at his doorstep instead of finding a pay phone to announce our visit. We were much more charming in person. Or at least less frightening.

"What are we gonna do after this doesn't work?" Tobey asked, walking up to the house.

"I have a good feeling," I said, ringing the doorbell.

"Just a second," a wonderful voice replied, old and crispy, with both joy and bite like Jimmy Stewart's, but mixed with a touch of Jew. I heard the noises of movement inside, and I thought about how "Touch of Jew" would be a good name for my signature fragrance. My mind wanders like that sometimes. Even when I have all of it.

A tall, thin man opened the door. The kind of old man

you dream of becoming: gray hair, balding just right up in the corners, but still with a tuft to comb up top. He was wearing a cardigan and corduroy pants, and I liked him instantly.

"I'm sorry to disturb you, sir," I said, "but would you happen to be Professor Leonards?"

"Yes, can I help you?"

"My name's Wayne Gladstone and this is my friend Brendan Tobey. We're hoping you could help us with our investigation into the Internet Apocalypse."

He wasn't pleased at the intrusion, and it was hard to blame him.

"Y'know, I do still keep some posted office hours at the university. This is my home," he said, closing the door.

"I'm sorry, sir," I said. "But we thought we'd have better luck at your home, and we already had the address." I extended the phone book until it was in his way.

The professor opened the door again and started to laugh.

"Well, I haven't seen one of these for a long time," he said.

He flipped the pages. "Where did you get this?"

"I'm sorry," I said. "I can't tell you that."

"Well, okay then." He handed it back to me and again began to close the door.

"We're the Internet Messiah!" Tobey shouted before it shut.

Another laugh. He had a great one. It rattled and built to a hum like some crank-driven machine.

"You're *both* the Messiah?"

"Okay, he is," Tobey admitted.

"The one from New York with that book?" he asked. "I saw a story on TV just yesterday."

I handed him his own copy of the journal in response.

"Well, you're quite the little lending library, aren't you?" he said and flipped the pages, but without the same interest he'd had in the phone book.

"Tell you what," he said finally. "I've decided it's more fun to trust you, but not in my home. I'm not that stupid. Let's do this on campus. You'll want to see the IMP anyway."

The professor drove us to campus in his Prius and that wasn't just a hostage prevention tactic. As a natural-born teacher, he wanted a captive audience for his lecture. Tobey kept trying to catch my eye from the backseat in disbelief, but I played it cool. I'd liked what I read about the professor, and I wasn't too surprised he'd take the opportunity to talk about his true love. Also, he was a bit of a subversive. He brought up the news story again, and it became clear that any enemy of the senator's was a friend of his.

He explained things I already knew from my reading, but it was better to hear it from him. In 1969, he was provided with a device known as the Interface Message Processor, or IMP, and he used it to supervise the connectivity between four computer networks at four separate campuses. It was called "internetworking."

"I was spot-checking," he said. "Basically, I was supposed to test the limits of performance."

Hearing the story for the first time, Tobey was more surprised. "You were figuring out how to break the Internet?"

"Well, no. Figuring out where it was breaking. How to make it work. Scientists build things."

"Yeah, like bombs," Tobey said, and the professor drove in discomfort for another half a block before pulling over to the side of the road.

"Wait a second," he said. "I can't believe I was so foolish. I thought you wanted a tutorial, but I'm really just a *suspect* in your little investigation?"

I wanted to say no. To say that I was positive the professor was a good man. And a lucky man, fortunate enough to be professionally brilliant for a living, because all that intelligence would have turned to anger if put to use in a factory or business. Instead, his soul was intact and vibrant in old age. I was jealous, but not in the way Tobey was, causing him to act out petulantly in the presence of a great mind. My envy was tempered by admiration because the professor clearly enjoyed sharing his knowledge.

"It's not personal, Professor. We were told that everyone in this phone book was a potential suspect. That this book, which started out representing who was online, changed and began to record who had power online."

"Let me see that again," he said, taking back the phone book. "1988?"

"Yeah. We're hoping to find more recent editions."

"I don't remember getting a book like this as late as 1988, and it's too small."

"Well, right," I said. "It's no longer a phone book. It's a listing of those with power," I repeated.

"Well, whoever made this in 1988 never gave it to me."

"That's okay," Tobey said, excited by an idea. "The fact that you didn't get it doesn't mean this book doesn't hold the VIPs of the Internet. It just means they didn't give it to you."

"Meaning?"

"Maybe it's not for you. I mean, look, you're the father of the Net. Of course, they're gonna have to include you, especially in 1988, when everything is still new. You're necessary."

Professor Leonards waited and watched me think. He saw me sizing him up. He saw me hearing Tobey.

"What are you thinking, Mr. Gladstone?" he asked.

"I think you're telling the truth, and I think my friend is right. The book is real, but at least in 1988, it still included people who knew how to make the machine work and not just those who sought to become its master."

"And that's the only kind of learning you hoped to do today? Is that right? That's the kind of investigation you're leading?" he asked.

"Yes," I said. "Is that bad?"

When you've lived long enough, you can turn disappointment into a smile, and the professor smiled. He wasn't going to give his typical birth-of-the-Internet show-and-tell speech today because for now our investigation was about people, not parts. But being a genius, he also found a way to give his lecture and answer my question at the same time.

"Y'know, Mr. Gladstone," he said, placing the phone book in my lap and giving it a tiny tap, "in the early days of the Internet, it ran on the existing network of telephone wires. We had to invent a communication protocol that accepted the limited power we had over those existing networks. Essentially, we developed a system of tolerated differences. We recognized the autonomy of our members. So you ask me if your methods are bad? I guess I'd say only if they keep you from connecting."

The professor drove us back to our car, and no one felt the need to talk further. We had our learning.

"It was an honor to meet you, Professor," I said, exiting his car.

He did not return the same compliment, but he did say, "I'm glad I got to meet you, Mr. Gladstone. Good luck with your investigation. And if it reaches a point where you do need some technical assistance, you may call on me."

"Y'know, I'm an idiot," I said. "I didn't even ask you if you have theories on who took it."

"Scientists always have theories, but nothing worth reporting right now, I'm afraid. I'm mostly retired. . . ."

I leaned in closer. Even Tobey was silent and respectful. We waited.

"I will say, however," he continued, "this is not a one man job. You know that, right? The Net is bigger than any one man. That's the whole point of the Net."

We drove back home and spent the rest of the day setting up a Messiah meeting at The Hash Tag. We posted fliers all around town, and then we stopped by a different FedEx Office (because Tobey was supposed to be at work) to make new copies of the journal. Understanding the importance of a brand, we also dubbed the journal *Notes from the Internet Apocalypse* and made copies on light blue paper, and left about twenty copies lying around town. Although that trend had actually already started, now we were explicit. Like Ziggy Stardust commanded listeners to play it at maximum volume, the book now instructed readers to place extra copies in places where like-minded people might read them. Libraries, buses, sexual supply shops. A new kind of manual retweet. And then there was the last page with its ongoing invitation:

Fans of *Notes from the Internet Apocalypse*?
Meet Gladstone and Tobey at The Hash Tag,
Santa Monica, Tuesdays at 7 p.m.
We'll discuss all things Internet Messiah and
how to bring back our Internet.

Tobey had decided on Tuesdays to mirror the date of 4Chan's meet ups at the Bowery Poetry Club back in New York. He wanted to make people feel like they were part of something. Acting out the novel in their way, and he encouraged me to go back to the brown sports jacket and fedora, which I refused to do. I'd be nervous enough without sweating my balls off in front of an audience. After several hours of promotion, we ended up at Apocalyptic Records in Culver City.

"I can't believe a Type A guy like you is going into your debut without a plan," he said, admiring a still-wrapped copy of Emerson, Lake & Palmer's *Brain Salad Surgery*. "What's the point of that?"

"I'll tell you," I said, "but first answer me a question: Why the hell would losing the Internet bring back records? Our downloads and CDs still play."

"Yeah, but you can't download new shit," Tobey said.

"Yeah, but these are *old* records, so . . ."

"See, this is what I'm saying. You're getting all analytical about the logic behind a used record store, but you're just gonna freestyle in front of new recruits? Also, you can't download old shit, either."

I stared at the cover of *Ziggy Stardust*. Bowie, still yellow haired and not yet a god, existing among the painted oil slicks and garbage outside K.West furriers.

"I have to see the people first," I said. "See what I'm dealing with. But the truth is . . . I have nothing to tell them. I can't give them a reason to follow me. They're gonna have to want to."

"That's bullshit. You can't just sell yourself. Even Jesus promised eternal life."

"Yeah and look where that got him," I said.

Around five, we drove back to Tobey's place and he let me take his car. I stopped by the liquor store, having heard enough about Hollywood Forever to know I might be needing it. One bottle of Jameson and one Grey Goose. Then I hit a Subway in Brentwood. The usual twelve-inch veggie delight on whole wheat for Romaya and a twelve-inch turkey and Swiss on Italian for me. Maybe she wouldn't be home. Maybe she wouldn't want to go, but I had to try, and worst case scenario, I had booze and sandwiches.

I remembered how to get to her apartment and I thought that was a good sign. The weather was nice, and that seemed auspicious too. I rang her doorbell, sandwiches under my arm, a bottle of vodka in my right hand, Jameson in the left. I could hear movement inside and I thought of a scenario that hadn't yet occurred to me: She could be home, but not alone. I took a step back, turning halfway from the door, just as I heard the deadbolt retract.

"Hi?" she said before looking down at the booze in my hands. "Um, sorry dude, the kegger's canceled. My parents ended up not going out of town."

"Oh, bummer," I said.

"Yeah. . . ."

And then our fun improv game was over. She was thirty-seven again, with her hair tied back and wearing a T-shirt, jeans, and no shoes.

"Are you okay?" she asked.

"Yeah, I'm great. Can I come in? Or, y'know if it's a bad time . . ."

"No, come in, I was just trying to send out more résumés, but it's hard because I feel really good about that Google thing."

Romaya walked into her apartment and it was much like it had been weeks before. Maybe a little messier, and I was glad I couldn't be blamed for the clutter. I sat on her couch and placed the bottles and food on her coffee table.

"So what's up?" she asked sitting cross-legged in her dining room chair.

"Have you ever been to Hollywood Forever?" I asked.

"What's that?"

"It's fun. It involves food and movies and booze. If you come with me, I can explain."

She didn't understand what was happening.

"I got you a toasted veggie sub on wheat," I said, holding up her sandwich.

"I heard Subway uses rubber in their bread," she said.

"Fuck, I dunno. Bring a gluten-free pita pocket and scoop the contents into it. Just come with me. It'll be fun. Promise." I picked up the bottle of Grey Goose to up the ante.

She stood up and looked at me hard, trying to see what was new. I was wearing jeans, sandals, the Son of Man/WiFi T-shirt I won at The Hash Tag, my *Miami Vice* sports jacket, and a fedora.

"You still dress like such a fucking asshole," she said and went to the other room, returning in flip-flops and a light sweater she'd had since college.

We took Tobey's car east on Wilshire and made our way to Hollywood Forever. I put the booze and food on the floor by her feet. I wanted to put my hand on her leg. That's what I would have done if we were still married. Or I would have held her hand. Squeezed it. And depending on what year it was, she would have squeezed back.

"Are those apartment buildings?" I asked.

"The Towers? Yeah, I guess you can live there. If you have an ungodly amount of money. So what's Hollywood Forever?"

"It's a cemetery," I said. "Where lots of movie people are buried."

"You're taking me to a cemetery?"

"Yeah, but the cool thing is, they show movies. They project old movies onto the wall of a massive mausoleum. And everyone picnics."

I turned to her as much as I could while still driving, and grabbed her hand to give it a shake. "I'm taking you to a cemetery that hosts movies and picnics, baby!"

She smiled and I let her go, before I could feel her not hold back.

"What's with the Jameson?" she asked. "No more Macallan?"

"You still haven't read my book, huh?"

"It's only been a day since you last asked. No, I didn't read your book last night after driving five hours from my Google interview."

"It's okay," I said. "Part of it's in the book. I started drinking Jameson because it was cheaper. I was out of the apartment for two months, searching New York City. Drinking in bars. It was a business decision. It's cheaper. Sweeter. Not as good."

"I see."

She was mad. I shouldn't have given her shit about the book again.

"And then I kind of broke myself. I got used to it."

"What do you mean?"

"Last week I was in some Santa Monica sports bar and I decided to treat myself to a Macallan for the first time in months, but I didn't like it. It was too smoky. Harsh. I'd lost the taste I'd acquired."

"So you drink Jameson now?"

"I guess, but that bottle's not for me. We're late. They line up for this place. I heard you can bribe yourself a spot in line with a bottle of booze."

She looked down at the vodka.

"Don't worry, Babe," I said. "The Grey Goose is yours."

Wilshire continued on as it does: The luxury apartments give way to porn offices that lead to foreign consulates without anyone noticing. And why should they? Those things can go together because everyone likes nice weather and only a handful can afford it. I cut north on

Highland, optimistic that I might actually navigate my way from Brentwood to Hollywood without fucking up. I wanted to do that. I wanted to be on Romaya's home turf without needing assistance. I wanted to be the master of everything, and so far so good.

"I think it's up here," I said. "In the town. We should look for parking."

I slowed down, looking for parking around shitty supermarkets and tiny takeaway taco joints.

"There's no lot?" Romaya asked.

I was about to say "don't think so," but I was surprised by a patch of vibrant green grass emerging from the surroundings, and I thought it was funny that the first thing to look alive among the cheap Californian markets and eateries was a repository for so much death. I kept that thought silent. Romaya didn't have to follow every turn of my mind tonight. It was enough that she associated my presence with comfort.

"Ooh, tacos," she said.

I wondered if that would have been a better call than Subway, but I had to stop doubting myself.

"Stop!" Romaya pointed. I hit the brakes way too hard, but she'd found a spot. "That old lady's pulling out from in front of the grocery store."

We parked and walked toward Hollywood Forever. I wasn't completely sure where I was going, but I wanted to lead Romaya anyway, and as we got closer, I saw a "No Parking" sign on a metal pole about fifteen yards away. I started timing my strides. Romaya was to my right, and

I was closer to the street, and without her noticing, I lined myself up with the pole as I turned my head to her, oblivious to everything in front of me. It should have been clear to her what I was doing, but it wasn't. That's how long it had been.

"So tell me," I said about two-and-half steps from the sign, "where else are you thinking of applying?"

"Well," she said, and I turned to the sign the second before impact, dramatically throwing my head back at the exact moment I kicked the base of the pole. The whole sign vibrated and shook with a perfect *dwang* as I staggered backwards and grabbed my skull to save my smacked head from crumbling to pieces. It was an old vaudeville trick, but still convincing if done right.

Romaya gasped in surprise before she remembered to laugh. A car slowed down to see if I were really injured and Romaya attended to me, excited to do another little improv. She placed one hand over her mouth and placed the other on my neck. The motorist's car window lowered, and I broke character to wave off his concern.

"You should have went with it," Romaya said.

"Why? I got what I wanted."

"Fooling him for just a second?"

"No, making you laugh."

Tobey hadn't misled me. There was a line, and Romaya and I walked along it until we found the person who we felt would most appreciate Jameson. Some twenty-something with an honest-to-goodness soul patch and sunglasses even though the sun had almost set. But just before I went in for the kill, it occurred to me that getting this guy's consent was not the same as getting the consent of everyone behind him. True, only the people directly behind this dude could see they were being cut, but still, I had no right. I wasn't sure why that hadn't occurred to me until now, and the last-minute realization wasn't enough for me to change course. The only thing I thought to do was perpetrate a further fraud. To cut the line in such a way that even the people behind my fuzzy, shaded friend wouldn't realize they'd been cut.

"Phillip?!" I said, knowing that no one present was old enough to appreciate the *Beverly Hills Cop* reference. "Phillip? Is that you?"

But before he could let the world know we weren't friends by speaking, I moved in close enough to whisper.

"I'd like to give you this bottle of Jameson if you let me stand here with you."

The dude, let's call him Phillip because I never learned his name, looked down at the Jameson and back up to me.

"Danny!" he said, and I passed him the bottle, patting him on the arm like an old friend.

"Sally," I said, turning to Romaya, "you know Phillip."

"Sure do!" she replied. "I never would have made it through calculus without him!"

And that's how we ended up securing maybe the most perfect spot to watch the movie. A perfectly executed deceit getting us something we didn't deserve. Better yet, the only people aware of our unfair placement were those responsible for giving it to us. Maybe I was just running a scam, but I remembered Hamilton Burke and thought he'd be proud of me for such tightly effectuated self-interest. Romaya loved it too.

We lay in the grass and ate our sandwiches. She knocked the vodka back straight from the bottle, and got a tipsy buzz within moments. She could do that. Get happy drunk almost instantly, and then drink more with no further effect. I could never keep up with her, but knowing I had to drive, I didn't have to.

Some people brought pizzas. Other couples came with lawn chairs and legit china in strong wicker baskets. Some had blankets. Some just sat in the grass like Romaya and me. We listened to the music and waited for the world to get dark enough to showcase the images revealed by light. Everyone was different and no one fought. And in this feeling of community, my act of cutting not only became more shameful, but more absurd. Almost unnecessary. "Oh, you got here late, dude? Sure, just step in. I think you need this more than I do."

Romaya kept changing position trying to get comfortable, and I was brave.

"Here," I said, and lay down behind her, placing my side against the small of her back. I patted my stomach while she contemplated the dangers of using her ex-husband as a pillow.

"Come on," I said. "I've been softening it up for you the last couple of years."

She laughed and settled into me, seeming comfortable for maybe the first time the entire night. I stroked her hair gently, at first. Really as more of a service to get it out of her face so she could see the movie. But as the first images flickered, I left my hand at the back of her head, holding the tiny curve of her skull, and I kept it there for all of Charlie Chaplin's *The Great Dictator*. My fingertips extending to her graceful dancer's neck while my thumb absentmindedly stroked her hair until she was sleeping. I wanted to wake her for Chaplin's speech, but she seemed content, and I wondered what she was dreaming as he said:

> **We have developed speed, but we have shut**
> **ourselves in. Machinery that gives abundance**
> **has left us in want. Our knowledge has made**
> **us cynical. Our cleverness, hard and unkind.**
> **We think too much and feel too little.**

She rolled over, still in a dream. Maybe a dream that took her back five years and asked, "Did you say something, babe?"

"No, nothing. Go back to sleep."

> **The aeroplane and the radio have brought us**
> **closer together. The very nature of these**
> **inventions cries out for the goodness in men—**
> **cries out for universal brotherhood—for the**
> **unity of us all.**

The movie ended and for a few moments, I lay there, pretending I was trying to wake Romaya, but really I was just stroking the darkness into her hair and remembering what it felt like not to be alone.

"Oh my God. Did I sleep through the whole thing?"

"Nearly. Let's get you home."

———

Romaya fell asleep again as we hit the road, or maybe just pretended to. I thought she might have been trying to perpetuate the moment safely. To exist further in the dream and that was all right with me. I pulled up to her place and she groaned as if waking up were too much to ask.

"Sleepy baby," I said and walked around to her side, opening her door.

She floated her hands out limply to me with half-closed eyes, like some kind of adorable zombie, and I planted myself firmly, taking her by the wrists to pull her from her seat with no sudden yank. She popped up, falling into me and running her hands down my back before settling on my waist. And when she opened her eyes she looked almost scared by arousal. The moon lit her in blue, and I remembered her on my law school dorm rooftop the night we picked that locked window and stared down at the luxury apartments across the way. We were still new. Just children spying on others' adult lives, oblivious to the hurt that would come.

But now maybe time had not only healed the wounds, but made us smart enough not to pick at scabs. I held Romaya under the same moon, but on a new coast, and she let me. More than that, she was holding me back. I wanted to say, "I still love you," but I didn't. I just kissed her, and she pulled me into her before standing up straight and backing me into the open passenger-side door. I placed a ghost of a left hand over the side of her right breast, before running it behind her back. I got scared when she moved, but she didn't pull away. She was getting her keys.

"Let's get you inside," she said,

I was thirty-seven years old and already getting hard just at the thought of having sex with my ex-wife. She opened her door and led me to her unmade bed, the mess exposed by the moonlight creeping through blinds. She turned before we reached the mattress, and I kissed her like before. Then I picked her up and threw her back onto the bed. She landed with a bounce and laughed, taking off her T-shirt and undoing her jeans. I pulled down from the ankles and she did that always-graceful two-second butt jump, allowing me to yank them off while she was in midair. I dropped my pants like a clumsy college kid and she lay back, waiting for me, half naked in broken light. And then it was just me and Romaya.

I climbed on top, straddling her waist and throwing off my jacket. Then my shirt. She started grinding from below, getting frustrated, and I liked that. I lowered myself close to her face and held her down by the wrists as I slid myself between her legs, teasing and working my body into hers. She wrapped her legs and we tormented each other with friction until she said something very dirty for Romaya: "Fuck me." And suddenly I thought of Oz and all the sex I thought I had and never did. I grabbed Romaya tighter, making sure she was real, making sure I was here. I kissed her too hard. I held her too tight. I leaned in further and she rubbed back at me.

"What did you say?" I asked, deep and warm in her ear, my scruff scratching at her neck.

"I said fuck me," she groaned, crushing me with her legs in frustration.

"Oh, yeah?" I asked and slapped her face quick and firm, the way I slapped Oz. I wanted to make her gasp twice—once from surprise and again when I was inside, but it didn't work out that way. She stopped on a dime, dropping her legs to the bed.

"What the *fuck* was that?" she asked.

I let go of her wrists and sat up. I didn't know what to say. Everything was broken.

"Is that how you've been fucking?" she asked, assuming, I guess, that only whores like to be slapped and only assholes slap them.

"I'm sorry. I got carried away," I said.

She considered me, watching me above her, deciding if everything had been ruined or if there were any way back.

"Come here," she whispered and I leaned in. Then she slapped me hard across the face. A good one. Much harder than the one I'd just given her, and I fell down laughing, holding my hand to my face, warm and throbbing. A ringing in my ears. She flipped me over on my back and got on top of me.

"Holy shit," I said still laughing. "Do you know how hard you just smacked me?"

"Oooh, yeah. Whips and chains, baby," she said bouncing on me playfully. "Soooo hot."

I let Romaya take control and watched the parallel lines of moonlight rise up and down her body, but this wasn't the reunion I wanted. She was too far away. I sat up, wrapping my arms around her, but that wasn't right either. Even with my face in her breast, it didn't feel like home.

"Lay back," I said, and supported her as she lowered back to the bed and I followed with her, but it still wasn't right. Even when I ran my arms under her back and wrapped my fingers up and around her shoulders. Even when she hooked her feet behind my knees, and I kissed her and kissed her. Even when the tension built until the release of love and pain. She tried to catch her breath and I fell to her side, my heart pounding. But even when I threw my arm over her like she was something I could never lose again, I knew I'd only had sex with Romaya instead of making love to my wife.

Tobey and I arrived at The Hash Tag at seven, greeted by a crowd that exceeded my expectations. Despite our meeting, the typical Hash Tag festivities had not been canceled, and that helped fill seats. Not everyone was here for me, but there were definitely some journals in the audience. Some in blue. Others in their original dog-eared white. And even better, there was cosplay happening. A handful of people were dressed as Internet Apocalypse "characters."

"Wow," I said. "It's you, me, and Oz!"

"Yeah," Tobey replied. "I bet you want to fuck two thirds of this audience."

I laughed, but Tobey had reminded me of the morning after with Romaya. I'd been holding it out of my line of sight for the last few days. Or, maybe more accurately, in my jacket pocket. Romaya woke before I did, just like she used to, but she didn't kiss my cheek or whisper in my ear. There was no attempt to wake her early morning playmate. She just got dressed, quietly, while I kept sleeping the way you do when you think you're being watched in safety. I had no idea I was dreaming alone while Romaya was changing into yoga pants and neon wristbands. It was the zip of her gym bag that woke me.

"Wow," I said. "And you give me shit for how I dress."

"It's for dance class," she said. "And I'm late. You can sleep, but please just lock the door behind you."

"You should have woken me," I said.

"You looked like you needed the rest."

"Yeah, but when are you coming back?"

She looked nervous, like my childhood memories of adults.

"I have to do a bunch of stuff. I'm going to get a new tire after the gym. I'm driving there on a donut."

I sat up in bed, and she put her gym bag on her shoulder.

"I put your clothes on the foot of the bed," she said, pointing to a neat little pile.

"One sec, I'll walk out with you," I said, grabbing my T-shirt.

"It's okay. Sleep."

I hopped into my jeans. "That's stupid. I don't want to be here without you."

She moved to the doorway, but waited for me, realizing she couldn't leave when I was seconds away from getting dressed. I put on my *Miami Vice* jacket, and something about that made her uncomfortable. She headed to the door of her apartment and I followed, stepping into my sandals along the way. She turned back to look at me before leaving.

"Careful with that jacket," she said. "I gave you back the letter."

I pulled it out and there it was. Again not where it belonged. I didn't understand.

"Well, what did you expect?" she asked. "You thought you could just sneak it into my Google shit and everything would be all right?"

I certainly couldn't argue with that, but I didn't have to. I had something better.

"But last night . . ."

She took a step outside so we were no longer in the same space.

"I had a really nice time," she said, "but . . ."

I walked outside and shut the door behind me, jiggling the handle to make sure it was locked.

"But?" I asked.

"I had a really nice time," she said again, and got into her car, and it didn't make me feel one bit better that she lowered her window and kept waving good-bye until she was completely out of sight.

Tobey found his tatted waitress friend Jynx and she sat us over at a reserved small side table, giving us a couple of Anchor Steams on the house. That was our reward for helping to fill the place with people. After about twenty minutes, she took one of the two mics set up on straight stands.

She was enthusiastic. "Welcome to The Hash Tag and the first official meeting for fans of *Notes from the Internet Apocalypse*!"

There was a giggle, and a twenty-something with those horrific ear plug things booed.

"Boo?" Jynx asked, unaccustomed to negativity.

"Just *Notes*," he said correcting. "It's cleaner."

"Oh, is that what we're calling it now?" Jynx asked, and looked over at Tobey and me. We shrugged. "Fair enough," she said. "So let me introduce one of your two hosts for the night—but before I do, I just want to remind you we got our liquor license back, so in addition to the flavored tobacco and beer, we're also selling booze! And now without further ado . . . Tobey!"

Tobey took over Jynx's mic, giving her a kiss on the cheek. "Thank you for coming," he said. "Before I bring up the man you might know as Gladstone or the Internet Messiah let me just say a few words . . . Butterfly. Earring. Frogurt."

The room was silent. I was silent. Then I got the joke. He had said a few words. Then some people in the audience got it too, but still, no one laughed. You couldn't have asked for a more awkward, moment-killing introduction. I stood up and straightened my white fedora. Tobey took the lifeline.

"Ladies and gentlemen, the Internet Messiah!"

About fifteen to twenty people in the crowd of fifty clapped enthusiastically, and I noticed a woman with cartoonishly long lashes, a short skirt, and horizontal striped stockings applauding with the kind of girlish fun that doesn't always accompany women with a bohemian fashion sense.

"Hello," I said and paused, unsure how to give my name. Back at the hospital, I'd learned to be a whole person again. More than a screen name. But I also knew that nothing about recovery required me to give everything of myself to strangers. And even though this was the real world, it was still very much like an online experience. Here was a group of like-minded strangers congregated around something they didn't fully understand. Something they had very little desire to fully understand, but something they wanted to be part of. Raised on the Internet, they were less trusting of television. Anderson Cooper couldn't tell them what the next thing was. It was the congregated buzz that told them I was it. They wanted to see it, be part of it, and it had to be a group decision. They wanted to be part of that herd.

"I'm Gladstone," I said, "and I'm looking for the Internet."

It wasn't until after the crowd applauded that I realized I'd just quoted myself from the book. But whereas 4Chan met that assertion with derision, these folks welcomed the possibility. Their applause faded with my smile and then there was nothing except the waiting for more good news. But I had nothing for this group of twenty-somethings yet except the Internet phone book in my backpack over at my table. And that was too important to divulge freely. Not everything is meant to be a tweet or Facebook post. Some details deserve private messages.

"So," I said. "I have some things to share, but I'd really like to get to know you all a bit first so—"

"Question," said the guy with the plugs. He raised his hand, keeping his arm straight and rigid while the rest of his body slumped in his chair, seemingly ashamed of that appendage's effort.

"Yes?"

"I read your book, journal, diary, whatever."

"And?"

"So, like, is it true?"

That was the obvious question and yet not the one I was expecting. "Well, it was the truth I knew at the time. I wasn't well," I said.

"Right, so no disrespect dude, but what part of being batshit makes you qualified to find the Internet?"

"That's the 'no disrespect' version?" Tobey asked. "What's the rude one? Same thing, but with more anal fisting?"

The crowd liked that. It was the Tobey they knew.

"I don't know," I said, talking directly to the kid, without anger. "I can't explain that to you. I just know that I've been in contact with Anonymous and gotten Jeeves' blessing. Tobey and I have been up to Google and UCLA recently. We're investigating, but we need help. If you believe in the cause, we'd like that help to come from you. I have nothing to sell."

A woman who looked to be in her mid-thirties was sitting off to the corner alone. Maybe it was her glass of white wine or her stylish glasses, but she seemed impossibly intelligent. "I have a bigger problem," she said, not quite raising her hand. It was more of a point.

"First of all, I'm sorry about your marriage and isolation and all that."

"Thank you."

"But there's something no one's talking about. Why do you even *want* to find the Internet?"

I didn't understand the question.

"I mean now," she clarified. "Why are you looking for it *now*? You're still the same guy who dumped all over the Internet in your journal, right? Just a way for millions of sad people to be alone together? You focused on every single negative, disgusting, dirty part of the Net, and now you're trying to bring it back?"

It was an interesting point, but interrupted by a pudgy kid at the front of the room who called out, "Hey, Tobey has black hair," he said pointing to the shag escaping Tobey's baseball hat.

"Yeah, I got that wrong in the book," I said.

"You don't even know your own friend's hair color?" he asked.

"Wait a second," a college girl two tables away interjected. "I thought Tobey was fake. Y'know, made up."

"No, that was Oz," pudge said.

"Listen," I said, with arms raised. "This isn't a book-club discussion. I need recruits. People to help with the investigation."

"I'm all for that," plugs said. "But why you? Just because you thought of it first?"

"FIRST!" another college kid shouted, raising his beer bottle with the label half off and flapping.

"Yeah, so why?" said plugs.

I didn't have an answer, but more importantly, I didn't want to give one. I didn't want to prove myself. I was me. I was here. Like jokes and love, my worth would be ruined if it had to be explained.

"So, no reason, then?" plugs concluded, and the room seemed to feel that was a fair conclusion. It was the shitty statement that would change the entire tenor of the comment thread. There would be piling on unless someone changed the flow again.

"Yeah, why you?" someone else called out. It was happening.

"Because he helped me," a woman said.

It was the long-lashed girl. She was standing now, and holding a blue copy of *Notes* under her arm like a Bible. I could see the black Cleopatra eye makeup creating the illusion of larger eyes. She might have dabbed some white in the corner, extending the sclera. That trick usually makes you look a little cross-eyed, but because her eyes were already set slightly further apart, it seemed to work out. Regardless, it wasn't the makeup that made her eyes look so huge. It was because she could hold all of me in her sight. She was seeing the man I'd hoped to be and wouldn't explain. The room went quiet, and I looked at her along with everyone else.

"Excuse me?" I asked.

"You helped me," she said.

"I'm sorry," I said. "Do I know you?"

"We were Facebook friends."

That didn't help. I had become Facebook friends with lots of people I didn't actually know. Mostly with people I didn't know. It's much better that way when you have no good news to post.

"I'm Alana," she said. "And I don't usually look like this. I'm dressed as Oz for tonight . . ."

She smiled, and I could see her now, even if I couldn't remember her last name. She saw me scanning drunken late-night memories for more.

"We met online like two years ago," she said. "Anyway, I was pretty depressed. I don't want to get into it, but you helped me, and I wanted to thank you. Although I guess I would like the Internet back, too."

If you're a functional alcoholic, it's easy to find the start of a lost weekend. It's usually Friday night. But e-addiction is more subtle. They used to call BlackBerrys crackberrys because of how often we'd check them, but by the time the iPhone rolled around there was no cute name for this affliction. Now, it was just something we did. And it was like that for me. A way to unwind de-volved into a way to see the world. I don't know when it went from a hobby to a way of life, but if you could some-how quantify the mess of my dropout, virtual life, Al-ana probably existed somewhere toward the start. The period shortly after Romaya left, when I was no longer going to work but not quite yet the near shut-in I'd be-come. She was a voice looking for help at the moment I threw my Scotch-laced self into comment threads and social media.

"I'm not sure how I helped you," I said. "But I'm glad."

"You listened," she said. "And you heard me when no one else would. When even my friends wouldn't listen."

I wondered if I were really that wonderful or if her friends were that awful. Probably neither was true. The Internet deserved the credit because in real life, the hard-est part about being there for someone is knowing once you extend the effort to make something right, once you take someone from sad to happy, from suicidal to safe, they might ask you to do it again. And again. And surely you run that risk online, but it's easier to say good-bye. People get blocked. They have their chat privileges re-moved. There are more buffers between you and a real connection, making it easier to say hello and good-bye. Distance makes it easier to answer cries for help, know-ing the Internet will never let your good deeds trap you into a pattern of selflessness.

Another man stood up. He was about my age, but had

a much kinder face than I do. "You helped me too," he said. Standing there in his cargo shorts and T-shirt, ten pounds too small, he didn't look familiar at all.

"I posted an adoption profile on Facebook when my wife and I were almost out of hope, and you shared it and even linked it on your Twitter."

I was not (as truly sad people call themselves) "Twitter Famous" but my steady stream of puns and off-color tweets mocking dead celebrities had amassed me a following of about seven thousand. Compared to someone with an actual life, that meant a lot more exposure, so I understood why he was grateful, even if I didn't remember the posting.

"Did that lead you to a baby?" I asked.

"No," he said. "The baby came about six months later, totally unrelated, but you have no idea how much it meant to my wife and me. Sometimes a kindness from someone you don't even know can mean the most."

"I'm glad. . . ." I lingered for his name.

"Ed."

"I'm glad, Ed. Will you help me bring back the Net?"

"Yes."

"Alana, will you help me bring back the Net?"

"Yes."

I addressed the whole room. "Do we have people here tonight who will help me find the Net?"

It wasn't a unanimous response by any means, but there was enough of a communal "yes" to be encouraged. I looked at Tobey, and he smiled back at me.

"Okay," I said. "Here's what's going to happen. As you might have guessed, and as my friend with the hideous body scarification earrings mentioned, Tobey and I are a couple of fuckups. Nevertheless, we've learned more than you'd think possible. We've obtained information we believe narrows the field of possible suspects. As you can understand, that's not something we're going to share freely to a room full of unknown drunken Californian assholes like you. We want to know you better, so if you came to help, I'd like to ask you line up over here toward the left wall."

People started to gather their drinks

"If, however, I dunno, you came to be part of some book club/cosplay fun and possibly have sex with Tobey, then hang to the right."

"Thank you!" Tobey said earnestly, like I'd finally remembered the key point of tonight's gathering.

"Not at all, sir," I replied. "So, I'm gonna leave it to you guys to police the lines, but Tobes and I are gonna sit at that bar there and drink and get to know you. You can come take a stool beside us one by one while we get your contact info and skill set. Cool?"

I didn't wait for a response. Spools and the smart lady had already thrown me enough with their questions. Now it was time to make executive decisions and hope others followed.

I took a step off the riser and as I headed to the bar made sure to pass by Alana's table. When she stood up I gestured, and she followed me to the bar, sitting beside me. So did Tobey.

"Be cool, man," I said, nodding to empty seats further down the bar, and he slid a few down, proud that he was being empowered as an equal to do the canvassing of new talent. The spools guy was the first person to sit next to him.

"Thank you for saving me out there," I said to Alana.

"That's what I should be saying to you," she said. "Can I buy you a drink?"

"Well, let's see what they have," I said scanning the shelves.

"Well, I was gonna buy you a Macallan," she said.

"Oh yeah?" I asked. "Even though I drank Jameson all through the book?"

"Well, yeah, but you explain that." She flagged down the bartender. "That was just, y'know, to keep expenses down. You were drinking Macallan at the start of the book and when we met on Facebook. You used to post about it."

It was hard not to be flattered by the attention to detail.

"Yeah, but here's the thing," I said. "A couple of weeks ago, I decided to treat myself to Macallan. And I didn't like it."

"Why not?"

"I dunno. I guess I just got used to the taste of the cheaper stuff."

Just then the bartender came up to us. "What can I get you folks?" he asked, and before I could speak, Alana put down her card and said, "Two Macallans, please."

Suddenly, I didn't feel flattered. I felt ignored, or at least misunderstood. But that happens sometimes when someone understands you better than you do.

Alana smiled at me and said, "Don't get used to the taste, Gladstone."

I felt the kind of warmth inside me that had recently only come from good Scotch. I would have held the moment, basked in it, but Alana's face suddenly turned from compassion to fear, her eyes growing as wide as her makeup's illusion. I turned around to see something I couldn't believe was real. It was Rowsdower, but now he wasn't all gussied up for some TV appearance. He was in action, wearing a tan suit and skinny tie with an immaculate knot. Perhaps most noticeable was his fedora right out of G-man central casting.

"Rowsdower," I said, unaware I was even speaking.

"Special Agent Rowsdower," he corrected, and flashed his badge inches from my face.

"Wayne Gladstone?" he asked.

"Yes."

"You have been declared a person of interest under the NET Recovery act. As such, I am empowered by the United States government to request you follow me for questioning. Will you be coming voluntarily or shall I place you formally under arrest?"

I didn't respond, and Rowsdower repeated himself.

"Will you be coming voluntarily or shall I place you formally under arrest?" he insisted.

"I thought I had a right to remain silent," I protested.

"You have no such right under the NET Recovery Act," he said, and in one fluid motion cuffed my hands behind my back before I could even think of a witty rejoinder.

Tobey jumped off his stool. "What the fuck, man?" he asked. "I thought this was America."

Rowsdower kept one hand tight on my cuffs and placed the other on Tobey's shoulder.

"The NET Recovery Act passed four months ago, son, and you're still talking about what *was* America. Please get out of my way. I have a job to do."

7.

My father retired just three weeks after I started working at the New York Workers' Compensation Bureau. It was as if Manhattan couldn't hold more than one working Gladstone at a time. He didn't mention that phenomenon during the one chance we had to meet for lunch. He just sat across from me eating his turkey club. No list of unfulfilled ambitions or impressive achievements was passed across the table. But for me it was still a changing of the guard, and I made a list for him, built from my memories and observations, and put it inside my coat pocket.

"That suit looks good on you," he said.

I rolled my eyes. "It's from Syms."

"Two for one?" he asked.

"Yeah."

He smiled. "That's always good."

Growing up, my father never shared a beer with me or taught me how to fire a gun. He barely drank, and hadn't touched a weapon since the Korean War. But I never felt deprived because I grew up in a house headed by a man who was always home unless he was working in the real world of New York City. He seemed the master of all the grown-up details that appeared far too numerous to be comprehended. My father could tell you where to park at the train station; where to stand on the platform for the doors to open; and which subway to take. He found his way home even when his train was canceled, and I would stare up in wonder, sure that if I were a grown-up, I'd stand in the middle of Penn Station crying in panic until I could give my name and address to a policeman.

He shaved every day—even on Saturday mornings—and I would scurry in and sit on the closed toilet seat beside him, waiting to be handed his electric Norelco razor and a tiny brush. He watched my fingers push back the tiny black tab that released the cover and offered encouragement as I worked the brush through the rollers and screens. I did a thorough job sweeping away yesterday's stubble and powder. It should have taken six seconds but I stretched the job out for a minute and furrowed my brow like a little Swiss watchmaker working delicate parts. He smiled while applying a thin film of powder from a squat round stick with a tiny plastic cover, and never rushed me.

When I was six, he showed me how to tie a tie. He taught me the full Windsor knot and gave me one of his ties to practice. You'd be surprised how many grown men can only tie a half Windsor. Half Windsors are quick and easy, but they're always crooked, even when tied correctly. I can tie a full Windsor, with no mirror, while waiting on a subway platform, and still get a dimple in the middle, just below the knot. My dad gave that to me, even though he ties half Windsors. And when I turned thirteen, he offered his electric razor, but taught me how to shave with an old-fashioned blade. I am not like my dad. I tie full Windsors, and buy disposable razors. But I am the choices he gave me. Some fathers can only teach you to be the man they are.

"Wake up, Gladstone," Rowsdower said and entered my cell. In one hand was a tiny stack table, in the other, a folding chair he'd brought before. He passed me the table and set the chair beside my cot. Then he took the table back and opened it between us.

"Ready," he called out over his shoulder, and a disgruntled guard came in with my lunch on a serving tray, dropping it on the table to destroy all the dignity Rowsdower was apparently trying to create.

That was prison in the Apocalypse. The NET Recovery Act allowed its enforcers a lot of freedom which was good and bad. It was a freedom that allowed Rowsdower the power to let me keep my real clothes, although the state was good enough to give me a couple of government-issue outfits. It was a freedom that let Rowsdower bring in unofficial furniture so he could sit down to watch me eat in my cell. And then there was my cell, which looked not at all like a cell. It was a room with a wooden door, and a wired glass window. It reminded me of high school. But the freedom was bad too, because without rules, a government is only as good as its people.

Rowsdower wasn't wearing his sports jacket today. Just a crisp white shirt with perfectly rolled up sleeves and a straight, navy blue tie.

"I wasn't sleeping, Rowsdower."

He paused. "Would it kill you to say my whole name: Special Agent Rowsdower?"

I shrugged.

"So, Mr. Gladstone," he said. "Let's go over it again."

It wasn't the first time we'd been through this. On the first day, Rowsdower was all business the way I'd remembered him in New York. I sat on my cot and he stood tall and thin in his gray suit and fedora, like some 1950s throwback. His anachronistic wardrobe seemed to be the one indulgence in his button-down life, and I had to laugh because even his tiny act of rebellion embraced the fashion of a more rigid time.

"Nice to see you again, Mr. Gladstone," he had said, staring at me in a way that revealed disbelief.

"Is this a social visit, Rowsdower? Because, y'know, we could hang out without you actually arresting me. How about bowling?"

"See, at this point, Gladstone, people are usually asking what their crime is. You've been here ten minutes and your first instinct is to be a dick. Why is that?"

I wanted to give a noble reason, but the truth was my wrists still hurt from the cuffs and it seemed defiance would ease that pain, but I wouldn't admit that. Not when there was a fight to be had.

"Why would I ask my crime?" I exclaimed. "You've already told me all about your NET Recovery Act. You can hold anyone indefinitely without counsel provided it's in furtherance of your investigation. You only need to tell me once."

"Oh good," he said. "I was afraid the message didn't sink in after all that Jameson and jerking off."

He threw one of Tobey's blue photocopies of my journal on the cot.

"I'm sorry," I said. "I'm not doing any signings today."

Rowsdower paced the cell for a moment before moving his fedora to the back of his head to open his face for conversation.

"Y'know, for the record," he said, "I may not be the best looking guy on the job, but I still don't think my head looks like a 'yellow laminated skull.'"

He gestured to my book. I forgot I'd written that and I felt bad. Rowsdower was thin, and there was something about his teeth that attracted more attention than normal, but he was not the emaciated attack dog I'd seen before.

"Sorry. Unreliable narrator," I shrugged.

"Also, it's not *my* NET Recovery Act. I didn't draft it, I didn't vote for it. Did you?"

"I didn't vote in the last election. . . ."

"Of course not. Why would the messiah of all e-humanity take an interest in politics?"

"Hey, look I—"

"Save it, Gladstone," he said. "It doesn't matter. This was passing in anyone's administration. The people want their Net. But as long as we're talking about it, do you understand what I'm empowered to do?"

I didn't speak. I had no lawyer. There was no charge. There was no process. Only the authority to find results.

"You out of jokes?" he said, walking over to my cot and standing over me. I stood up too, feeling too defenseless, but that only made it worse because Rowsdower had a good four inches on me even when I was standing.

"Why don't you tell me what you know about the Net?" he said.

And that's how it went. Just like that for weeks. The constant intimation of danger, but no torture. Rowsdower would ask me questions about the disappearance of the Net, what role I played, who my associates were, and what information I had gathered. And I told him everything except my association with Quiffmonster and his gift of the Internet phone book. Not only had I made a secret of the only valuable thing I knew, but I was suppressing the only evidence I had that I was a man capable of accomplishing anything. Without that phone book, I had no clues. I had nothing to show for my efforts. Nothing cemented my mission as real except the faith of a growing number of strangers.

"So that's it?" he asked. "You got nothing? You stood in front of that room of fans to tell them nothing? To give them nothing? Why the fuck do you write everything down if you have nothing to say? You're as bad as the millennials. Do you think the world will stop spinning if you don't record your every fucking thought?"

"I don't understand," I said. "I saw you on the news. I thought you knew I didn't know anything."

"Frankly, Gladstone," he said, "I don't know what you know or don't know. I just said that to shut up Senator Bitchface, but, yes, the powers that be have taken an interest in you, and you need to tell me something quick."

"Why?"

"Because I don't *like* it here."

"Sorry to hear that Rowsdower. Have you tried harassing some prisoners down the hall?"

"I don't mean here, with you. I mean L.A. They called me up because I met you already in New York. They brought me here . . . because of you."

"Oh. . . ."

"I don't like being asked if I prefer egg whites when I order breakfast. Do you understand? I miss the subway. I don't like the traffic, the smiles. I don't like the *sun*, Gladstone. You might be okay shitting away your life in a room, but I am *not* okay watching you do it in Los Angeles. So, y'know, if you're gonna be useless and quiet, wanna do it in New York so I can go the fuck home?"

There was something I did want to tell Rowsdower. Something that had plagued me since Bellevue.

"I have a confession Special Agent Rowsdower," I said.

He waited.

"Back in New York I told you my wife was dead. She's not dead. I'm sorry. I know that now. I was just . . . off."

"I know, Gladstone."

"You know?"

"Yeah, I know. I know everything. I knew it then. And even if I hadn't read your journal and done, y'know, my job, I'd still know."

I didn't respond and he continued.

"Maybe because it's in your file. Maybe because I'm the hand of the most powerful government in the world, authorized with tremendous power to get results. Or maybe it's because she's waiting to see you right now."

It had been weeks since I last saw Romaya or even spoke to anyone in depth. I was starting to hope Rowsdower would just beat the information out of me so that I'd spill everything and this could all be over. But maybe he knew what he was doing. Maybe he realized I was only good at sitting alone in a room when there was available liquor and functioning WiFi. Now I was antsy and eager.

Despite the million chirping voices pecking at my skull for freedom, I tried to stay cool. I wanted Romaya to see me self-possessed. I wasn't sure if I should change into street clothes, but ultimately decided to throw on my sports jacket and fedora over my blue prison attire. It created a look not too dissimilar to the jacket/scrubs ensemble I sported when I first hit L.A.

Unlike my cell, the visitors' room looked very much like my prison expectations. There were several segregated stations with opposing seats, glass, and telephone receiver. Romaya waited for me behind glass, unsure of where she was or what she'd see. And for reasons I don't understand, that insecurity inspired me to act as if I were right at home. I sat across from her, greeting her like a guest, and nonchalantly grabbed the phone as if I'd done it countless times. As if anyone else had come to see me.

"How did dance class go?" I asked.

"What?"

"I haven't seen you since your class. Everything turn out all right?"

She ignored the question.

"I came to see you at Tobey's," she said.

"Why?"

"I wanted to thank you."

"What for?"

"For driving me to Google," she said. "I really appreciate it. I even got you a present, but I guess I can't give it to you now."

She pointed to the little tiny slot in the glass. A plastic tray like the kind you could pay a nervous New York City taxi driver through. The guard in her corner of the room took notice and moved a half step closer.

"Too big?" I asked.

"Yeah," she said. "I don't even know why I brought it. Stupid."

She reached down to her side before reappearing "Here."

Romaya presented me with a three-quarter-liter bottle of Jameson.

"Jameson," I said.

"Yeah."

I thought about Alana at The Hash Tag, and how Rowsdower had arrived before I got to drink the Macallan she bought me. I thought about the thick sweetness of Jameson rolling over my tongue.

"What?" Romaya asked. "I thought this is what you like now."

"Yes. You're right," I said. "Thank you. That's great."

"I'll give it to you when you get out." She paused and stared at my clothes. "When *are* you getting out?"

"I don't know, Romaya," I said. "I'm a person of interest under the NET Recovery Act. They have questions. They can keep me indefinitcly if they want to. Do what they like."

"Do you have a lawyer?" she asked, and I laughed.

"Something funny?"

Nothing was funny. She wasn't visiting her husband. I was just a man she knew, seemingly not even as well as strange women in bars did.

"I'm not entitled to a lawyer under the NET Recovery Act," I said.

"Oh. . . . I read your book."

I stopped being hurt and petulant for a moment and looked at her again, wondering if she'd seen behind the journal's booze and sex. Seen how much I still loved her.

"And?" I asked.

She paused. She considered the tiny slot in the glass between us.

"Well . . . I guess I didn't realize things had gotten so bad for you."

I laughed again, still without meaning to. "Yeah. Pretty bad. . . . So. Anything else? I know you're busy."

"Yeah," she said. "You got some mail. I don't know how they found me, but it's for you. Just sent to me. In care of me. It's from workers' compensation," she said, and turned to the guard. "Can I push this through?"

He came over and opened my mail in front of me without hesitation.

"Now you've gone too far," I said. "Jail people indefinitely without counsel for no articulated crime, sure. But opening someone else's mail is a federal offense, buddy."

Romaya looked at me. He didn't. Neither of them laughed. He also didn't care enough to read the letter. He just made sure it contained no contraband and gave it back to Romaya. She thanked him and folded it in half before passing it through the slot. I took it from the slot and pressed my love letter flat against the glass in front of her face.

"Trade?" I asked, and she put her head down. "Guess

not." I put the love letter back in my pocket and took the workers' compensation letter.

"What does it say?" she asked.

"It doesn't matter. They're gonna cut off my disability payments."

"What?"

Back before my hospitalization, all I had to do was show up once a month and talk to some shrink who checked a box and kept my half salary coming, but Kreigsman had insisted on seeing me every week in light of the whole jumping-off-the-ferry thing. He was clear about it. Insistent. But I came to California anyway. And that was months ago.

"I haven't seen a psychiatrist for a while," I said. "I have to get back to New York by next week or they're canceling my benefits."

"Maybe you can work it out so you can see one here," she said.

"Maybe. But hey, at least food and shelter's currently being provided by the state."

"I don't think you should ignore that."

"Okay."

"I'm serious."

"Okay, I won't."

I waited for her to say we had fun on our date and that we should do it again when I got out. And after waiting in silence, I swallowed the last bit of pride an unloved prisoner can have and said, "I had a good time at Hollywood Forever."

"Me too."

"Did you forget we could?"

"No. I remembered."

"Good luck with Google, Romaya. Thanks for the mail."

I turned to my guard and signaled for the door without looking back. I didn't need to. I knew the precise image I wouldn't see.

They brought me back to my cell, and I lay there for a while with no interruptions. When Rowsdower did return he was a different man. Every fanged instinct of attack disappeared when he closed his mouth, and I noticed he actually had a kind face.

"You enjoy your peep show, Rowsdower?" I asked, referring to my exchange with Romaya, all of which was no doubt recorded.

"Not so much," he said. "No offense, but I like to see more of a performance from women behind glass."

I laughed and wondered if I was coming down with Stockholm syndrome.

"We're sending you home, Gladstone," he said.

"What? Just like that?"

"Just like that. It's been three weeks. You gonna miss me, Tiger?"

"I'm happy to leave, but I don't understand."

"To tell you the truth, Mr. Gladstone, neither do I, but there's this thing in the world you've forgotten about. It's called a boss. I have one, and boss says it's time for you to go."

"Your boss is incredibly wise and sexy."

Rowsdower threw open my door and repeated himself. "Time to go," he said.

"Should I give back the clothes?" I asked.

"I wouldn't dream of ruining that ensemble. Take the clothes, compliments of the government."

I paused in the doorway. "I'm glad you get to go back home, Special Agent Rowsdower," I said.

"Thanks, Gladstone. But can I ask you to do something for me?"

"Yeah?"

"When you do get out there. Try to do something worth getting arrested for."

8.

I hadn't seen Tobey in three weeks, but once again, when needed, he was somehow reachable again, even if I did have to borrow a phone. Apparently, even under the NET Recovery Act I was entitled to a phone call, and the phone I was offered belonged to an incredibly bored middle-aged woman sitting behind a semicircle of Formica in the middle of what could only be called an office-building lobby. She rested the unit up on the ledge and turned it to me. This was not a prison.

I walked outside freely for the first time in three weeks, and headed to the corner of Sepulveda and Wilshire, as Tobey had suggested. A guard saw me out and pointed the way. I had apparently been held at the L.A. Veterans Affairs building, which with its tall white walls looked far more foreboding than the name would imply. I reached the corner, and in only thirty minutes, Tobey was there.

"Gladstone, lose that fucking hat!" he said, lowering his window.

"Very funny." I walked to the car.

"No, I'm serious." He held up a pair of cheap sunglasses. "And put these on. We need to keep you out of sight."

"Uh, Tobes, not for nothing, but they just released me. I think I'm safe."

I buckled up, noticing something was different, and it wasn't just the newfound cleanliness of Tobey's car. My words weren't bouncing off Tobey the same way. He was alert. Motivated. Normally, I would have spent more time figuring out what catalyzed the change, but I had too many things on my mind and I didn't want anything to get in the way of the colossal *fuck you* I was about to deliver. I even took off my hat and put on the shades so he'd have no distractions.

"Thanks for coming to see me in prison, asshole," I said. "I mean, I thought maybe I was in a secret location or not allowed visitors or something, but Romaya showed up today. You couldn't manage?"

Tobey smiled his different smile. "I'm sorry, G-Balls. But I couldn't come to see you. A lot's changed in three weeks. For starters," he said, reaching for the backseat, "check out your book."

Tobey pulled a fresh photocopy from my old backpack and handed it to me. I was relieved to see he'd had the presence of mind to grab the pack after my arrest, especially considering it had the Internet phone book in it.

"Pretty great, right?" Tobey asked.

The book looked fantastic. Now it was velo-bound, blue, and most impressive, it had cover art. Right in the middle was a drawing of a WiFi signal wearing a fedora. But not just any fedora. The curves leading up to the pinch were thicker, more emphasized, and clearly in the shape of an "M":

"You drew this?" I asked.

"Yeah." Tobey was prouder than I'd ever seen him.

"Is that supposed to be an 'M' in the hat?"

"Yep!"

"Does that stand for me?" I asked.

"Close. The 'M' is for 'Messiah.'"

"That's what I meant, fuckwad," I said, and Tobey laughed.

"It's awesome."

"Yeah, well that's just the start," he said.

We headed east on Wilshire toward the Farmers Market, where Tobey insisted I'd see something that would make everything clearer. He also explained that the movement really took hold after my arrest. There was now a more immediate cause than getting the Internet back: "Free the Messiah." That was the goal and the next Hash Tag meeting was flooded with people dying to join the cause. And not just addicted-Net zombies jonesing for their fix, but people with skills. Apparently people claiming to be affiliated with Anonymous were stopping by, but there were also all the MMORPG guys missing the adrenaline rush of their online gaming, willing to perform a host of tasks to satisfy their crushing need for high-risk kicks. But even more important was a whole contingent of employees from high-profile Web-based companies who no longer felt secure in the continued existence of their jobs during this Apocalypse. It made them bold. It made them do things. According to Tobey, a group of Facebook employees showed up at The Hash Tag two weeks ago, delivering some intelligence.

"What do you mean 'intelligence'?" I asked.

"Grab my laptop," he said. "It's in your backpack."

I pulled Tobey's computer out of my bag, relieved to see the Internet phone book still safe inside. Then I opened it up.

"Facebook has stuff on everyone," he said. "Stuff on you and on me. Well, at least they did. Look." Tobey felt around his neck where he was wearing two thumb drives like necklaces. He took one off and handed it to me.

"A gift from our new recruits."

"When did we stop calling them disciples?"

Tobey didn't reply, and I inserted the flash drive into his computer, waiting to see Facebook's data on me as the video player fired up. I was not prepared for what I saw.

"Jesus Christ! What the fuck, Tobes?!" I asked. "That's where I sleep now!"

Tobey laughed and then he stopped laughing. "Wait, what?" He turned the laptop so he could see the screen and was greeted by video of himself sitting pantsless on his couch, jerking off to his webcam.

"Oh fuck," he said yanking out the flash drive. "Wrong one."

He took the other drive from his neck and handed it to me. "This one's you," he said.

"This data really comes from Facebook?" I asked.

"Yes. They save everything. And not just the text. Any time you've used their webcam function, they've got a record of it. And anything you've done on that cam. And maybe even data when you didn't know you were being recorded . . ."

I put the flash drive in my pocket for later and closed the computer.

"But even if that's true, what does that have to do with bringing back the Internet?"

"Well," Tobey said. "Maybe we should consider what we're bringing back."

"So you sent your new recruits to find out?"

"No, they came with that. I think they wanted to show what they can do for us."

"And what can they do?" I asked.

"Well for one, they could destroy all of Facebook's ill-gotten data before we bring the whole thing back online."

"That's not our mission," I said. "We should be looking for suspects." I pulled out the Internet phone book and flipped the pages in Tobey's face. "Have you looked at any more of these names since I was locked up?"

Tobey kept driving.

"Wait, is that why you didn't visit me?" I asked. "So I wouldn't get in the way of your new missions?"

"Not at all," Tobey said. "When you got locked up,

things really started happening for us. You became an icon. A symbol."

"So?"

"So I wanted to keep that going. Y'know, you're locked up, no one has seen you, no one has heard from you. I wanted you to be some big fictitious symbol like Guy Fawkes or Che Guevara."

"Those were real people!"

"Even better," Tobey said. "Anyway, the martyr angle is working because people already know you from the book. They know Gladstone is really good at suffering. It's like your superpower."

We pulled up to an outdoor mall that Tobey called The Grove and parked in a main lot.

"What I have to show you is in the Farmers Market," he said.

We passed food stands with meats on sticks and falafels and organic produce. One dude was selling rubber bouncy balls that lit up on contact, and I had to drop five bucks to get one because three weeks in fake jail makes you crazy for whimsy.

Tobey led me in the direction of a white clock tower and I followed, bouncing my ball, and hoping each flash of light would illuminate what was wrong, because my spidey-sense was tingling.

"Look at this side," Tobey said and pointed up at the clock tower. There, right under the clock and a sign reading FARMERS MARKET was Tobey's Messiah symbol, thirty feet wide: WiFi wearing an M-shaped fedora. And underneath it, the words "Free the Messiah."

"Holy shit."

"That's right," he said. "These have started popping up

all around town in the last few days, but this one's the biggest. We had some Halo-loving douchebags do it in the middle of the night. Called it a covert painting op to give them a kick."

I stared at the graffiti, impressed but uneasy.

"Yeah, but why fuck up this market?" I said. "I like it. Look at this neat ball I got here."

"Because it has to exist beyond a book jacket, Gladstone. It's the symbol of our movement. And people have to see it. I can't share it on the Internet. That's the point."

I stared at the symbol some more and Tobey let me stare, waiting. "But I'm not imprisoned. I'm free," I said, finally.

"Well, I don't think anyone needs to know that. That's why I told you to lose the hat and put on the sunglasses. You made the cause legit by being locked up."

"I'm not gonna pretend to be in prison, you psycho."

Just then some market workers came with ladders and whitewash to address the vandalism. I was glad. I wanted to see them heal the tower.

"Fuckers," Tobey said.

A tall thin man worked his brush over "Messiah" first.

"Well, there goes that," Tobey said, as a streak of white was pushed straight across "Free the Messiah."

"Looks kind of like a blank now," I said.

"Yeah, that's their point. They're gonna make it disappear."

"No," I said. "I mean like a fill in the blank. It doesn't have to say 'Free the Messiah.' It could say anything."

"Like what?"

"Anything anyone wants to say about the cause."

I had Tobey's attention for the first time all day.

"In fact, you should start adding, like, ten of these symbols in the back of the book, with a dotted cutting line and blank lines above and below the image."

"Like a meme?"

"Exactly like a meme. Let the disciples write their messages above and below the image, and drop them around town. Let them define the cause. Who I am isn't important. I'm just the guy in the fedora. Let the symbol be their inkblot."

"That is a great fucking idea. Maybe you *are* the Messiah."

I smiled a too-proud smile.

"What?" Tobey asked, prying.

I bounced my ball one more time, and then looked up. "More like the Meme-siah, amirite?"

Tobey got really happy the way friends do when they know you've just created a shared moment to be recalled later, and I felt we were back on the same page. I put my hand on his shoulder, and he pulled me in for a hug. But that's that thing about hugs: even when two people are together, they're facing opposite directions, staring at different things. If Tobey weren't looking the wrong way over my shoulder he would have seen what I saw: an approaching old-fashioned trolley. A quaint reminder of an earlier time which someone in California had resurrected and monetized for tourists. I watched it approach. And then I watched it explode.

Fire darted out from behind the first car along with a sound that hit me in the chest, seemingly unshielded by Tobey. We fell to the ground, divided. The front car had been blown from the tracks and onto its side, but the second car continued running along its tracks, burning. I pulled Tobey up and hobbled away from its trajectory. There was smoke and the awful sound of metal grinding against concrete. Worse than awful. Useless, because the screeching violence of rock and steel did not conceal the screaming. Not just the screams of spectators like Tobey and me, running aimless and afraid, but screams from inside the trolley. Screams of pain and the screams of those seeing the pain.

I was scared, but I walked back toward the suffering. At least I took a step in the right direction. I wasn't sure I was brave enough to see more. There was a man, about forty, on what was now the first trolley car, his eyes darting around the market.

"You," he said to me. "Please!"

And I went to him because how could you not? One step became two and then there was a jog that broke into a run because the man's eyes required nothing less. I got to the trolley, and there was a boy on the floor. About ten years old. There was blood everywhere, especially in a puddle beside him, and I saw why. Most of his left arm was in it.

"You're a doctor, right?" the father said, gesturing vaguely to my blue scrub-like prison uniform and my white sports jacket.

"Tobey!" I screamed. "Get over here."

I took off my jacket and knelt down to the boy, who was very white and not breathing right.

"Hey buddy," I said. "I want to show you something, but I have to do something first, okay?"

I grabbed the sleeve of my jacket and tied it around his arm. Hard. He moaned.

"Almost over, buddy," I said. ·

I pulled it even tighter and tied it again so it would stay. The rest of the jacket draped over the stump, hiding the injury.

"Hey, Dad," I said to the man. "Could you just hold this and maybe apply some pressure?"

I heard an ambulance, and I was glad because I was now officially out of ideas. Tobey was running to us.

"Get that ambulance here!" I screamed to him.

I knelt back down to the boy. "Hey, look. I got you something," I said, and handed him the ball. "Can you take it?" I asked pressing it into his right hand. He was weak, but he closed his fingers on it and smiled for a second. He had dirty-blond hair long enough to move when he blinked. His lips were chapped. "It lights up."

I heard the sound of medics running.

Tobey was standing over us now, and I took my backpack from his shoulder, removing the Internet phone book. I stared at the boy's dismembered arm on the floor and remembered being in my backyard when I was about his age. I'd helped my dad put down some pesticide/fertilizer stuff on the lawn, and when we were done there was still two thirds of this stuff in an incredibly heavy vinyl-like sack. My father asked me to put it in the shed, but I was tired, and the mulch pile was closer. It wasn't like me, but when he went inside, I dragged the bag into the mulch where it sank into grass clippings and leaves. I helped it sink, kicking more leaves over it, and made a note to remember where I'd left it, for next year. I remembered in fall when the leaves further buried it and I remembered when it snowed. In the spring, I knew my father would come looking, and one weekend, while he was at the hardware store, I went to dig it up and drag it to the shed like I should have in the first place. I remembered exactly where to go and if I hadn't, I still would have known because now, right on top of where I was headed was a dead squirrel. It wasn't like the roadkill I'd seen from the safety of a speeding car. It had gotten into the fertilizer and died a horrible death. Its body was frozen in convulsion like some hack actor's portrayal of death, and a grimace had formed by the exposed teeth of his half-rotten face. I could not look directly at it. I could not touch it.

I lined a trash can with a garbage bag and put it right up to where my peripheral vision said the squirrel was. Then I dug blindly with my head turned. I wanted to grab a clump of leaves and dirt and squirrel all in one motion and dump it away. It took several tries, but when the shovel felt heavy enough and the garbage thud sounded right, I turned my head fully to make sure it was gone, before tying up the garbage bag and throwing it away. Then I dug down to the pesticide and pulled it to the shed, ignoring the tiny teeth and claw marks where he'd burrowed into his death.

There was no time for such half measures now. I made sure the boy was looking at the ball, and then in one motion, I grabbed the arm by the wrist and put it stump first into my backpack. I zipped it up and handed the backpack to the father.

"The ambulance is here," I said to him.

He called over my shoulder, "Here! My boy is here!"

We watched them put the boy on a stretcher, and a paramedic tied a real tourniquet just above my handiwork. He threw my jacket on the floor before whispering to the father, who gestured to the backpack. And then they were gone. I grabbed my jacket, suddenly remembering it still held my letter to Romaya, now bloody. I put it in between the pages of the Internet phone book to blot it out, and folded my jacket into a square. There were more people than just the boy. Some dead or burned, some with just minor injuries. But no one else thought I was a doctor. Now I just looked like a convict covered in other people's blood.

Tobey drove while I lay in the passenger seat, reclined all the way back. I wanted to go home, but I didn't know where that was. It wasn't Tobey's apartment. It wasn't back in New York. I wasn't even sure it was here with Romaya. Maybe I was trying to claw my way back into something that would kill me. Tobey was right. I needed a place to hide, but not from the authorities—from everything I'd seen. Everything I'd touched.

We pulled into a space in his apartment garage, but were pinned by a limo as soon as he parked. The black tinted glass rolled down with mechanical efficiency, revealing a man in a Hellraiser Pinhead mask. "Get in the car, jackasses."

"Quiff?" I asked.

"Do you know many other masked men roaming around in limos, Gladstone?"

It was Quiff, but before I could I decide if I wanted to enter, Tobey was inside, sticking his head out the window right next to Pinhead. "Dude, come on, there's a wet bar and everything."

I got in and the car began to move.

"Eventful first day out of prison, Gladstone?"

"Yeah, man, it was awful," Tobey replied.

I turned to Tobey. "You know Quiff?"

"Of course," he said. "I told you Anonymous pitched in when you went to the big house."

The car pulled out of Tobey's garage and out into Santa Monica.

"So, Gladstone," Quiff said. "What happens now?"

"What do you mean?" I asked.

He shook his head. "If you're gonna be the Messiah, Gladstone, you need to think more than no moves ahead. This is chess, not Ants in the Pants."

"I told you, I wasn't looking for war."

"And I told you it would find you anyway, didn't I?"

I had no clever reply.

"So I'm asking you," he continued. "What happens now?"

"I don't understand."

Even through Halloween-store latex, I could tell Quiff was disgusted with me. "Driver, turn on the news," he shouted.

Quiff sat back in his seat and listened to a news story he'd already heard in his head. One I hadn't even begun to imagine. It was about the explosion at the Farmers Market. That much was no surprise, but clearly that wasn't the important part. It was the ending. The part about the newly formed Internet Reclamation Movement, now seemingly called the Messiah Movement, being suspected in the attack.

"What the fuck?!" I screamed.

"You didn't see that coming?" Quiff replied.

"Because it's not true," I protested. "Is it? Is it true, To-bey?"

Tobey was drinking some of Quiff's vodka. "What? No. I didn't order anyone to blow up a fucking trolley," he said.

Quiff turned professorial. "But what does that matter? A trolley blew up. And in the shadow of your WiFi/fedora symbol—which is really nice, by the way."

I reached for the Scotch and Quiff interrupted me by placing an empty glass in my hand. Then he poured me some Auchentoshan Classic, which was behind the decanter I was actually grabbing for.

"You're a suspect, Gladstone," he said. "So tell me. What happens next?"

"Well driving around with Anonymous/4Chan/Whatever the fuck you are can't be a very good idea. It makes me look guilty."

"That's probably true, but the association is already known. Enough to paint you as guilty if they want, so I'd suggest you need all the friends you can get at this point. Friends you can trust."

"Oh, right. Friends like masked vigilantes known to me only by a dirty joke of a nickname?"

"I *AM* the Batman," Tobey said.

"I've explained this to you already," Quiff said. "In this environment, the man in a mask is the only person you can trust. Everyone else has too much to lose."

"Okay, Quiff, so what happens next? You tell me."

"You will be blamed," he said. "You will be discredited. And you will be vilified."

Then, almost by cue, my old friend Senator Bramson came on the radio.

"I've been warning this administration and anyone who will listen about this so-called messiah for months. And for good reason. Look what this movement has done. And what does this administration have to show for it?"

I knocked back my drink and put my head in my hands, running my fingers over my face and through my hair like I'd seen exasperated men do.

"We'll figure this out, Gladstone," Tobey offered weakly.

"Cheer up," Quiff said. "Don't you realize Senator Bramson just became your best friend?"

"Ooh, with benefits?" Tobey asked.

"Shut up, Tobey."

"Yes," Quiff agreed. "Take a break, Tobey. We get it. You're a moron."

"How is she my friend?" I asked.

"Well, think about it: She's blaming the NSA. The NSA just released you. So—"

"I was being held by the NSA?" I asked.

"Who did you think?" Quiff asked.

"Well, I dunno. That Rowsdower seemed like such an FBI guy."

"He is. Was. But he's been tasked as a foot soldier in the NSA's effectuation of the NET Recovery Act. So anyway. If Bramson is blaming you, the NSA has two choices: They can arrest you again and try to bury the fact that they ever let you go. Or they can dispute Bramson's allegations, which means you won't be blamed. We have to get you on TV. Deny any involvement. Condemn the attacks. Help the government help you, because y'know, if they do need you to be the bad guy for this, then nothing can help you."

"You think that's all it takes? Go on TV and say, 'Hey, I have nothing to do with this?'"

"Well, think about it. You'll be so grateful to the U.S. government for not wielding its NET Recovery Act power on your ass for something you didn't do, you'll keep your nose clean. Think of it as a get-out-of-jail-free card."

"But that's bullshit," Tobey said. "This movement goes on. And if they lock up Gladstone, we'll only grow stronger."

"Hey, good for you Tobey!" Quiff said.

I hated everything about Quiff's tone, but I also knew he was right.

"So, no," Quiff continued. "I think you should go on TV, but I don't think it's enough. It's a stopgap. It saves your ass for now and allows the government to save face, but you'll be compromised and they will never stop planning your destruction, because if they lock you up again, Tobey's right, that buys them another problem. But for now, yes, going on TV will work."

"Why so sure?" I asked. "You think I'm that charismatic that no one will doubt my performance? You think the government will take comfort from that?"

Quiff laughed. "No, Gladstone, you're probably right. If the government had to rely on that alone they'd probably be more nervous, but I think they have another ace up their sleeve. Any guesses?"

Tobey thought hard. "Aliens?"

"Tell us," I said.

"The Internet. I predict within the week the Net will make a temporary return. Just enough to quell unrest."

"What does that get them?" Tobey asked.

"What does that get them?" Quiff barked. "How can you of all people ask that? Indifference. Apathy. It gets them that. You've had the most motivated productive month of your life without the Internet! It's Governance 101. A content people are the least likely to rebel."

"I thought that was the purpose of religion," Tobey said.

"Yes, that too," Quiff agreed.

"Professional sports," I offered.

"Right again. These are the things that make capitalism work. The things that make you take your eyes off how the system is rigged to fuck the common man on behalf of the elite. You might be working more and more for less, but hey, wasn't that World Cup exciting? And don't worry, you'll go to heaven ultimately while the rich burn in hell, so take comfort in that."

"I feel like we've gone off-topic here. . . ."

"Not at all," Quiff insisted. "Because religion, sports? They don't have a thing on the Internet."

"It's bigger than Jesus," Tobey smirked.

"Bigger than Jesus, the Beatles, and Elvis combined. You can steal content for free! You can communicate without long-distance charges. You can zone out and do nothing while feeling like you're doing something for hours, days, your whole life. Why am I explaining this to you, Gladstone? I read your book."

I sat forward in my seat. I got close enough to Quiff to see his eyes were blue like mine. Blue like that not-Net creature I'd imagined in the Statue of Liberty at the end of my New York investigation.

"What's wrong?" Quiff asked.

"Nothing, I just hate it. I hate this. Why does everything have to be just . . . fuck."

Quiff turned to Tobey, who nodded in agreement. "What he said."

"Look, I know the Net was created by geniuses in conjunction with the military," I said. "But can't it just be a symbol of our ingenuity instead of just another form of control? Can't it just be a pure thing?"

"Like what?" Quiff asked? "Nuclear power that can solve the world's energy concerns with just an occasional Chernobyl? Or television that can bring Shakespeare plays into people's homes, as well as attack ads during presidential campaigns? Grow up, Gladstone. There are no pure things. People are dirty."

I thought back to college. Romaya had taken a job at a mall Starbuck's kiosk before quitting due to all the sexual harassment coming from her ecstasy-chomping hippie boss. I'd come to pick her up too early one day. I was always too early, but this day I used the time to wander the mall.

I wasn't looking to buy anything with just twelve dollars in my wallet and too little in my checking account to make a twenty-dollar minimum withdrawal, but I saw a dollar store and wondered if I might find something stupid and fun to give her. Before I entered, I saw a father with three girls, all with tidy, clipped, ridiculously blond hair, walking toward the store. His T-shirt and jeans were stained, and I assumed he had a job that didn't require him to shave every day. Despite having girls looking to be about ages twelve, ten, and eight, he couldn't have been more than thirty.

The girls were leading the way, but before they entered, they stopped and looked back at their dad, who said proudly, "All right, girls. You can have anything you want!" They squealed and ran into the store like contestants on a shopping-spree game show.

"What's choking you up, Gladstone?" Quiff asked, but I didn't answer. How could I explain to him what I'd seen? How could I tell him about a father who had nothing, but found a way to create a moment of unbridled joy for his children? Were there words to describe the hope, or at least the possibility, of this man patching together enough tiny moments so that by the time his girls realized how desperately poor they were, they'd already have had a happy childhood? Or could I explain what this father must have felt knowing that, in a world trying to crush him with everything he didn't have, for this moment, he was a hero? How could I explain any of that to a man who didn't believe in pure things?

"I don't think I can explain it to you, Quiff," I said. "I believe in pure things."

"I know you do, Gladstone. You're a true believer, and that's why going on TV isn't enough. After you do that, you'll have a choice to make. You'll have to stop your investigation and go away, or raise a real army and shut this whole thing down. You find the latest Internet phone book, narrow your lists of suspects, and I'll help you raise forces for attack."

"Wait a second," Tobey said. "If you think the government can just turn the Net back on, doesn't that also mean you think the government shut it off? I thought we didn't know who was responsible. I thought that was the point of finding the newest Internet phone book: to limit the list of suspects to just a few."

Quiff paused for a second. "Yes, good point, but everything is connected always. No one can sustain anything without some form of collaboration. Now it's time to gather your forces. It's a matter of survival."

"I don't want an army. I don't want to fight anyone."

"What do you want?"

"I want to explain. I want to teach. I want to sit with even a man like you, steeped in pragmatism, and explain that pure things exist."

"You'll be sitting a long time, Gladstone."

"Well, then I want to go home. Take me home. I have no idea where you've taken me."

"You are home," Quiff said, unlocking the doors. I looked out the windows for the first time to see we were right outside Tobey's apartment. "We were just circling while we talked."

I got up to leave without saying good-bye.

"Gladstone," Quiff said, handing me a blank business card with a handwritten phone number. "Promise to call me when you need that army?"

Part III

9.

I never believed I was anointed. Not really. But sometimes, if I didn't think too much about it, I did feel watched
over. Even as a child. I guess it's just a form of narcissism
to believe the world puts things in a certain order for your
eventual success. It's like the people who say everything
happens for a reason. If I examine that thought, I find it
both absurd and repellent. But if I don't think about it at
all, then yes, that time you run late because you've mis-
placed your keys, then miss your plane that crashes . . .
sure, it's hard to not feel like someone is trying to tell
you something.

Leaving Quiff's car, however, I felt none of that. I felt
like I was on my own and nothing short of more work
than I was capable of would change my future. Even with
Tobey walking beside me, I felt alone. Even worse, I felt
my heart and lungs and ribs existing in my body. The
physical signs of a panic attack. Dr. Kreigsman had taught

me to recognize them. They say knowing is half the battle, but they don't tell you there is no second half, and fifty percent of anything is never a solution.

So it was with as much comfort as surprise that we found Jeeves sitting in Tobey's doorway reading *Fangoria* magazine. (The Apocalypse had been so good to print.)

"Jeeves, what the . . . "

He got to his feet with a bit of effort and held out his arms for a hug. I put my head on his shoulder and hugged him tight and squishy.

"What are you doing here?" I asked.

"It seems you need me," he said.

"Yeah, but this all just happened. How could you get here so fast?"

"Came yesterday. Felt it coming."

Tobey interrupted. "Um, Sylvia Browne, if you knew it was coming, how about calling in a tip?"

"No, prick, I didn't know about the trolley. Just that Gladstone might need me."

Nothing good ever happened in Tobey's apartment, and I didn't want to go inside. I had a better chance of avoiding the panic if we kept moving, so I suggested we get into Tobey's Matrix and take a drive. Tobey picked Mulholland Drive, and Jeeves and I clung to our door handles as Tobey took turns with too much confidence, tempting the Santa Monica Mountains.

"I thought this would cheer you up, Gladstone," he said. "Y'see, L.A.'s like two cities at least. There's L.A.—y'know Beverly Hills, Venice, and all that—and then there's The Valley. You can see both from up here."

He addressed the last part of the narrative to the rearview mirror because Jeeves and I were in the backseat.

"Can you watch the road?" Jeeves asked.

"We're high enough to look down on it now, but all that smog and pollution that releases to the ocean on the L.A. side just sits in The Valley. Also, it's, like, always ten degrees hotter."

"Why would that cheer me up?" I asked.

"Because, y'know, the Lynch movie, *Mulholland Drive*? Remember that hot lesbian scene with Naomi Watts?"

Tobey pulled off Mulholland and headed south, turning right on Highland.

"Hey, the Hollywood sign," Jeeves said.

I hated to admit it, but I always wanted to see that up close.

"Who built that?" I asked Tobey.

"I don't know," Tobey said.

"And why?"

"Um, still don't know?"

"Yeah, I should research that," Jeeves said, and we looked at him. "In a *library*. Y'know, I do still know how to do that."

With the sightseeing and fear of imminent death over, we started bringing Jeeves up to speed as he looked us over with increasing incredulity.

"Yeah, it's a lot to believe, huh?" I asked.

"No, that's not what you're seeing, Gladstone. If I understand you correctly, you basically have one clue. A list of suspects in some Internet phone book."

"Yes," I said, handing it over to him. "Can you feel anything from it?"

"No, I can't feel anything from it, but that's not the point," he said, and then turned still and confused.

"What is it?"

"You," he said. "You look different." He stared and then looked down at my hat on the seat between us before placing it on my head. "Ah, there you are," he said with a surprising amount of relief. "There's my Messiah."

He smiled and straightened the hat before remembering he was annoyed with me. "Oh, anyway, the point is you're looking for the most recent version of this phone book so you can further narrow the search, right?"

"Yes."

"That's the part that's killing me. Am I correct that you've still done no actual research on the names in this book? I mean some of these people might be dead now. Some might have formed corporations together. There are connections. Clues."

"Well, in my defense," I said, "yeah, we started. We visited a former UCLA professor from the book, but that's when I got locked up. I've been held by the NSA for the last three weeks."

"And what's your excuse?" Jeeves asked, turning to Tobey, but he didn't wait for an answer. It wouldn't have been good anyway. "Tell you what," Jeeves said. "Give me that phone book and take me to a library. A real one."

Jeeves had made us feel equal parts shame and gratitude, so after we dropped him off at UCLA we set about making our contribution: preparing for an emergency Messiah meeting to address the Farmers Market explosion. By now it was midafternoon and we had only a few hours to get it together for that night. Fortunately, in my time away, Tobey had practically become royalty over at The

Hash Tag. Along with my book, he'd elevated a hack drug den masquerading as an Apocalypse party place to ground zero for the Messiah Movement. So he arranged an impromptu "Messiah Release Party," and we made fliers beseeching followers to call their friends. We also stressed calls to anyone they knew in the media. The Hash Tag liked that. With no Internet, being on the news was just about the coolest thing there was.

"I still think we should get Anonymous involved," Tobey said while stapling a flier to a telephone pole.

"Who? Quiff? Isn't he 4Chan anyway? Why do we call him Anonymous?"

"Because who knows? There's a fine line between defenders of liberty and pranking jackasses."

We showed up at 8:30 P.M., which we felt would give us enough time to fill a room—or at least fill the first few tables near the stage so it would look like a full room if the media came. There was a line down the street. Jynx busted out of the door and kissed Tobey right on the lips.

"You did it, baby! I'm gonna make mad tips tonight."

Another change from the last few weeks. He hadn't even mentioned they were dating.

"Gladstone," Tobey said, "you know Jynx."

"How are you?" I asked.

"Great. Good luck with the show tonight. There's, like, five different networks here! I'm gonna be on T.V.!"

"Exciting."

"Hey, you changed your outfit," she said.

"Oh, yeah. The old one had kinda had it."

I didn't bother reclaiming the white sports jacket after the paramedic episode. I thought about appearing in my prison clothes, but that would send the wrong message. So before the show, I stopped back at the apartment to throw on jeans, a T-shirt, and my old brown corduroy sports jacket. It looked kinda worse for wear after the dip in the Hudson River, and was far too hot, but I wanted to be recognized. Also, I still needed a jacket pocket to carry my love letter to Romaya. Then I swapped the white fedora for the old brown one so I'd match, because even guys who dress like assholes have standards.

Tobey and I took our spot as we had before, only this time our free drinks were a Scotch for me and the most expensive beer the bar kept, Radeburger, for Tobey. People stared like we were celebrities, but they did not approach. I wondered about that, but then I noticed a truly terrifying six-foot-four bouncer standing behind our table.

"Gus," Tobey called to him. "Say hello to my friend Gladstone. He jumped off the Staten Island Ferry to find the Internet."

"Evening," Gus said without uncrossing his arms or taking his eyes off the crowd.

"The dude's fucking unflappable," Tobey said.

Jynx took to the stage and played to the cameras in a way that made me incredibly uncomfortable.

"Say you want a revolution?!" she shouted, and everyone hooted and hollered because if we hadn't, holy shit, the douche chills would have been unbearable.

"All right," Tobey said. "But she's really nice and a freak in bed. And, oh, by the way, I told her to just introduce you tonight. It's your night."

"Before I bring up our special guest, straight from his

NET Recovery Act arrest, I urge you to try some of our special drinks. There is The Messiah, which comes in two versions, an $8 Jameson and a $12 Macallan. There's also The Tobey, which is just PBR in a can, except you call it The Tobey. Sorry. I thought of that one. And The Oz, which is a Foster's because that's Australian for beer, mate, even though I understand that no one actually drinks Foster's in Australia. But still, y'know?"

Tobey was deeply embarrassed.

"So here he is. You might know him as the Messiah, but to us, he's just Gladstone!"

I was greeted by the loudest ovation of my life, and none of it felt personal.

"Thank you," I said, and the applause did not die down. I waited. I watched the cameras zoom in.

"I don't have a lot to say. I understand this is a bar. I understand we're all united in a cause. I understand that we're celebrating my release from an undeserved incarceration, but today is a day of mourning. People died today. I saw people die today. As you know, something dark and evil blew up a trolley at the Farmers Market. That order did not come from me. It did not come from anyone I know, and if anyone here committed murder today under the twisted notion that it somehow supports our cause, then leave. This organization wants no part of you."

I took a candle from the front table.

"I know this doesn't change anything or mean anything, but I'd like us all to pray. To pray that the wounded heal and to pray for those who lost people today, that they find strength to continue."

I closed my eyes and lowered my head, raising the candle high.

"What is this, fucking church?" a voice called out. I looked up and saw some kid with a shaggy haircut, shaved at the sides, and a neck tat. "I don't need to hear some messiah talking about God."

"Did that sound smarter in your head before you said it out loud?" I asked.

"You know what I mean. Save that shit for Senator Bramson."

"Look, I'm not sure God exists either, but we're saying a prayer, and if you need to believe in something better and more important than yourself to join us, then why not look at every other person in this room who had the decency to keep their mouth shut?"

I lowered my head again and thought of all I'd seen wounded. I thought of the boy and wondered if reattaching that arm was at all possible. I thought about the squirrel I killed in my backyard. And after a minute, I thanked everyone and returned the candle.

"That's mostly what I had to say tonight. Tonight can't be about anything else."

"Can it be about the five more reported dead from an explosion in San Francisco twenty minutes ago?" a reporter by a cameraman asked.

"I don't know what you're talking about."

"I just got off the phone with my breaking-news editor. Right at this bar. He called to tell me a bomb went off in a San Francisco movie theater today. Five already reported dead."

"I have no idea. That has nothing . . . why would . . .

why would you even think that has anything to do with the Internet Reclamation Movement?"

"There was a WiFi hat symbol on the wall outside the theater."

"That's it? No. I know nothing about that. And I don't see how murdering Americans would help us get the Net back, turn back the awful NET Recovery Act, or get me out of prison, as I'm already free."

There was no answer and the cameraman just kept filming. Everyone was waiting.

"Well, the only other thing I have prepared for tonight is this: Tobey, hand out the memes."

Tobey sent out three sets of photocopies to the crowd, all with the image of the M-shaped fedora-wearing WiFi, with blanks for writing above and below.

"The paper you're receiving is the symbol of our organization and it was drawn by idiot savant Brendan Tobey over there. Some of you have been spray-painting it around town with the words 'Free the Messiah.' Well, there's only two things wrong with that: One, I'm free, and, more importantly, I'm not the Messiah. We are the Messiah. This is our organization. And we decide what the message is. So go ahead, take a paper meme and make it your own and spread it around. Make more. Leave it everywhere. In your classrooms, on your doors, on workplace bulletin boards. On walls. Spread what the Web is to you and why you want it back."

There was silence and confusion. There was the sound of skepticism, which is silence plus tiny movements.

"This is a movement of words. Of thoughts and ideas. But what I'm asking you to do is to write something pure.

Boil the Internet down to the purest most valuable thing it offers you and spread that around."

The skepticism remained.

"I am not the Messiah. This is the Messiah," I said taking off my fedora. "And anyone can wear this hat who believes in pure things."

"So the Messiah's a hipster douchebag?" the guy with the neck tat said, getting some laughs.

I ignored it. "Well, friends, when there's more to report, we'll report. But it's been a busy day, so that's all . . . for now."

I knew it was time to leave. Slowly, calmly, but now. Seeming indifferent to the crowd's disappointment was the best defense to being called a failure. I had to rise above and let it sink in. I didn't have a car, I still didn't know my way around L.A., but I walked out into the night and took my hat with me. There was some faint applause and chatter as I hit the doorway, and I kept walking. It didn't matter where. All that mattered was removing myself and leaving words in my place.

No one followed. Not Tobey. Not Alana, who I didn't even see in the audience. Not the reporters. No one. And as I turned a corner, I could just barely hear Jynx say, "For the next thirty minutes, two-dollar Tobeys!"

For the first time in our weeks together Tobey woke me. He dropped a copy of the L.A. *Times* on my head.

"You made the front page, Gladballs," he said.

"You're up early," I said.

"I haven't been asleep yet. I just came from Jynx's and saw the paper."

I looked at the headline: "'Meme-Siah' Denies Involvement in Farmers Market Bombing."

"Fuckers took my joke," I said.

"Yeah, congrats. You're as funny as the *LA Times*," Tobey replied.

Just then, Tobey's phone rang. Neither of us were used to that. He went over to the kitchen to pick it up.

"Hello," he said, and somehow that seemed wrong, as if technology affixed to a wall required a more formal greeting.

"Oh, hi," he said. "Uh huh. Uh huh. Well, yes, right, that is the address. Great."

He was about to hang up before bringing the receiver back quickly to his face. "Quick question," he said. "Can I come too? Okay. Awesome."

"Who was that?" I asked.

"We have ten minutes to get dressed. There's a car outside waiting to take us to the Playboy Mansion."

That certainly didn't seem like an obvious thing to be told, but ten minutes later Tobey and I were in the back of a limo arguing.

"I can't believe you didn't wear a bathing suit," he said.

"I'm not going swimming," I said. "Besides, they invited the Messiah. I might as well play the part." That sounded like a pretty good excuse for wearing jeans, scrubs, and a corduroy sports jacket with a matching river-beaten fedora.

"Good point," Tobey said. "Why would you want an outfit that would allow you to hop in a pool with Playmates?"

The car pulled into the estate and I saw all the assorted

displays of wealth and success you'd expect. But the car didn't stop near the pools or tennis courts. Instead, it carried on until we reached a place devoid of anything you'd associate with the Playboy Mansion. We were let out at what looked like a tame country-club buffet. There were serving stations, a jazz trio, and waitresses going around with hors d'oeuvres. Attractive women to be sure, but still appropriately dressed in clothing that must have been too warm for the weather.

"I don't see a pool, Tobes, but maybe you can take a dip in a fondue fountain or something."

"What the fuck is this?" he asked.

Just then a woman in her thirties introduced herself, but I didn't catch the name. Maybe Hugh Hefner's daughter. I thought I'd heard he'd had a daughter. I wasn't sure.

"Welcome to the Playboy Mansion," she said. "We're all excited you're here. Please, make yourself at home."

"Thank you," I said, and wondered if Hef would be making an appearance. Tobey had said the invitation was extended on the phone directly on behalf of Hefner himself, but I didn't risk seeming uncouth by asking.

"Where's Hef?" Tobey asked.

"Don't worry, Mr. Tobey," she said. "He's always around. Um, would you care for a change of clothes? . . ."

I laughed, and then felt bad because it seemed to be one of the few times Tobey was actually embarrassed.

"Actually, could I get one?" a twenty-something with ridiculously manicured hair asked. Like Tobey, he was in a bathing suit and tank top. His tan was immaculate and he had clearly paid someone to ensure that his pubes never escaped his skimpy suit. He looked familiar, but I couldn't place him. Some star of Disney movies or WB television shows.

"'Sup dude," Tobey said. "Loved you in that thing."

I wasn't sure if Tobey was also blanking or if that was the cool way to give compliments here. In any event, their instant rapport and similar dress gave our hostess an idea.

"Y'know," she said, "would you guys prefer to be by the pool?"

"Awesome," the actor replied, as if that were a response, and I felt disappointed. Grabbing a crepe and a mimosa was all I had in me at the moment.

"You don't mind, hanging back here with us, do you Mr. Gladstone?"

I was relieved. "No. Not at all." I turned to Tobey and the actor. "You kids have fun."

Tobey and his newfound friend followed an escort toward some wholesome smut destination, and I headed for the bar. No one stared at me for being freakishly underdressed. Or at least they were too well-bred to let me catch them staring. I stood in line behind a man, clearly fidgeting with something, and waited for him to order before realizing he already had. He just wasn't good at getting out of the way. I ordered a mimosa because I thought that's what people at these things drank. I hadn't actually had one since my mom let me take a sip of hers at some Disney World hotel when I was a kid. It seemed to be a normal order, and when the bartender delivered it with a slight over-reveal of cleavage in an otherwise wholly appropriate black-and-white ensemble, I wondered if she'd worked her way up from bunny.

I handed her a two-dollar tip and started my search

for a table when I heard a voice say, "You don't tip at a free bar."

It was the fidgety man from next to me. He turned around and I saw his agitation was just his efforts to properly cut his cigar.

"I know," I said. "But bartenders work for tips."

"Okay," he said. "But how much is 20 percent of zero?" He lit his cigar and exhaled straight up into the air above him.

I thought I might know this man, especially since he was wearing the kind of slow smile that meant he recognized me. He watched me work through my awkward half knowledge. And nothing about my struggle quickened his pulse or influenced him to relieve my confusion a second sooner than he wanted to.

"Can I offer you a cigar, Mr. Gladstone?" he asked, and then I could see him clearly.

"Hamilton?" I asked.

"There you go," he said. "But in business, the parties usually make a mutual decision to go by first names."

"No offense, sir," I said. "But to tell you the truth, I've forgotten your last name."

That, of course, wasn't true. I remembered Hamilton and had insisted to Kreigsman that he was real. Now I had my proof, and he offered me the cigar I'd not yet accepted.

"I'm sorry I can't offer you a Cuban," he said, "but I only have three and I want all of them."

This time I was the one who laughed, and I accepted the inferior offering gladly. I followed him to a table he'd already commandeered before my entrance.

"So," he said. "Things are looking up for you since last we met."

"How so?" I asked.

"Well, you've amassed a movement and, more importantly, you've gone . . . what do they call it? . . . paper-viral?'"

"Oh. Most of that was accidental," I said, and saw him frown almost disapprovingly. Once again, with just the slightest expression, he was able to fill me with shame like few men could. But I didn't want to embarrass myself as I had in New York. I didn't want to brag, and most of all I didn't want to show my hand. He wouldn't respect me if I did and I didn't want to lose that. He was rich, powerful, and successful, but he was the one talking to me.

"I suppose you're just spilling with ideas on how to monetize it?" I said.

"Oh, a few, yes. You're in the right town to get it optioned for a movie."

"I want to, Hamilton," I said. "But who could they cast to play a man as sexy as you?" He smiled and patted the skin under his chin with the back of his hand like a fading matinee idol, but he didn't laugh. I was quick to follow. "Also, I didn't write the book for money. I was just holding my head together. You know that. And now it means something more."

I could see he was about to ask just what it meant, but I was sane. I was sober. He could not dictate now. "What brings you to L.A.?" I asked, changing the subject.

"Money," he replied, and I had to remember that only the incredibly rich are not deeply embarrassed by the transparent pursuit of wealth.

"Sure," I said, "but I guess I just didn't see you as a Playboy Mansion kind of guy."

"Look around. Is that what this is? I'm just spending some time with old friends. And new ones."

He raised his Scotch to my mimosa. I clinked his glass and looked around.

He was right. I would never know I was at the Playboy Mansion. Of course, nowhere in L.A. seemed real to me. The whole place felt like the paint was still drying.

"This town doesn't have New York's history, huh?" I asked.

"It will," he smiled. "You just have to give it time."

I laughed. "I didn't realize you were funny," I said.

"Oh, thank you." Hamilton seemed pleased to add my compliment to his collection. "So, what brings you here?"

The question brought a stark reality I hadn't expected. What was I doing here? I could tell Hamilton Tobey got a call, but even Tobey wasn't with me now, and Hamilton was the only person speaking to me at what was purportedly the Playboy Mansion. I'd read my book. I knew this could mean there was an excellent chance I'd suffered a major setback. None of this seemed real on paper. Still, I could feel my chair against my back. I could see the tiny mole resting in the wrinkle by the side of Hamilton's eye. There was a level of detail that didn't feel like delusion. Maybe I was crazy, but maybe I was finally strong enough to accept a larger truth.

"Well, Hamilton, if you'd asked me an hour ago, I don't know what I would have said. But what brought me here? I'm starting to think . . . it was you."

"Is it that obvious?" he asked, and clinked my mimosa

again. "Oh, this is ridiculous." He called over to the bartender. "Get this man one of what I'm drinking." He turned his attention back to me. "Don't worry. It's on Playboy," he said. "Old friends."

The bartender brought me a Scotch neat, and after one sip it took all my strength not to reveal that too much had just happened in my mouth. Warmth and science and nature had commingled for the purpose of instructing me that the very best Scotches are orgasms made for men who can no longer come.

Hamilton smiled. "Yes, you're my guest. My plus one, so to speak."

"You arranged all this for me?" I asked.

"No?" He laughed. "Who the fuck are you? I was just in L.A., visiting friends, and saw you on the news. I thought it would be fun to see you. Also, I enjoyed our section of your book and thought you might miss me."

"Thank you," I said, and remembered I had a cigar burning in my hand.

"Seriously, you should sell it. It's not like you couldn't use the money. I would think that's your ticket, no?"

"I didn't come to L.A. for a ticket, Mr. Burke. I came for my wife."

"Yes, I read that. And how's that going? Deliver your letter?"

He'd got me speaking again. Proving myself, and I didn't like it. I stood up from the table and finished the rest of my Scotch in one tilt, which was a foolish act of defiance, akin to shoving half a filet mignon down your throat.

"You've been very gracious," I said, "but I'm afraid I have to cut our reunion short."

"I didn't mean to upset you," he said.

"Not at all," I replied. "There are just things I'm looking for, and I won't find them getting drunk with you."

"Ah, the Internet," he said.

"That's one."

"Well then, I won't keep you," he said. "Happy hunting. This is California, after all. There's gold in them thar hills."

10.

Truth is stranger than fiction. But it has terrible pacing problems. You can wait and wait for something magical to break the confines of your dreams, and it might come. But even if you get to meet the wizard, you never recover all the time you lost waiting.

Things come in bunches after a long nothing because life needs life to happen. Each event carries an energy-seeking cluster that brings things to a boil. Sometimes the water absorbs the warmth of one flame with only the smallest of bubbles losing their grip on the bottom of the pot. And if that's all there is, you might never predict that with just one more candle, the water would thrash and jump the rim, looking for something more than the shape of its surroundings.

There was no way of knowing today would be a day like that. And perhaps I'd hoped to make it *not* happen, believing a contemplated life remained still, like a watched pot. But Romaya came in the morning and she brought a letter. Not my love letter, which still lived unwanted in my jacket pocket, but another letter she received on my behalf. When I opened the door I could see she was eager to be released of its burden. Or at least that's what I thought I was seeing.

"What's wrong?" I asked, but she just handed the letter to me and stepped inside. It seemed the State of New York wanted me to know that in furtherance of its prior correspondence, and due to my failure to attend the mandated psychiatric appointments that were a condition of my disability compensation, all payments had now ceased.

"It's fine," I said, and put the letter in my pocket.

"What's fine?" she asked. "What will you live on?"

"I'll figure it out," I said. "Don't worry. I won't try to crash on your couch."

"Don't be an asshole," she said. "I'm not worried about that."

I took a step closer, holding her gently at the wrist. "Wait. Does this mean I can crash on your couch?"

"Oh fuck off." She pushed me away.

"Y'know, you would have laughed at that once," I said.

"So?"

"Okay, Babe. You got the job done. Letter delivered. And message received. You don't want me around, so why do you give a fuck about my financial standing?"

Romaya looked confused, but I wasn't sure if it was confusion stemming from the answer or how I could even ask the question.

"We were together over ten years," she said.

"Yeah, and now we're not. And you want it that way, so . . . so?"

I knew my argument was logical, but if sounded petty. Maybe more to me than to Romaya, because she was thinking about something else. Something bigger than us.

I sat in the back of the Matrix, and let Jeeves take shotgun. We were headed for the Oakwood Apartments, so Tobey took Santa Monica Boulevard east through West L.A. The apartments were allegedly home to former child actors, porno stars, and at one time, Rick James, but that's just what Tobey told us because he didn't have a blog to spill it on. Other than its location, nothing about the place was important. We weren't going inside.

Tobey crossed Wilshire and I guess we were in Beverly Hills because Tobey said "Beverly Hills" and Jeeves looked around harder than I would have ever expected. Maybe his cynicism had vanished for a moment, but I didn't care. There were galleries I'd never go to and stores I'd never have the money to shop in. What was there to see? I almost enjoyed the fact that we were cruising Beverly Hills in a ten-year-old Matrix, and wondered if the beautiful people would think we didn't belong or wonder if the vehicle belonged to an idiosyncratic celebrity. Of course both options were stupid. We were invisible.

There was a nice stretch of green on the left. A park I guess. A buffer between the street and the large homes beyond it.

"How much to own one of those?" Jeeves asked.

"Not as much as the ones higher up," Tobey said without even turning his head.

I walked to the couch and offered Romaya a seat beside me. It was all I had, and it occurred to me I actually had more when I was in jail.

"I'm sorry," I said. "That was shitty. What else is wrong?"

"Where's Tobey?" she asked.

"Asleep for hours, I'm sure," I said. "He doesn't work Sundays."

She sat down, and that's when I remembered.

"Oh, shit," I said. "Is this about Google? I'm sorry I didn't ask. What happened?"

"No," she said. "I'm still hoping to hear. Called, but they said they're still at the start of the process."

A few years earlier, I would have pressed her, but not now. Maybe I'd learned something, or maybe I was just tired. I waited from a distance, and it was as if my pulling back made enough space for Romaya to lift her head and look at me.

"I'm pregnant," she said.

"Pregnant?" I asked. "Is it . . ."

"Of course it's yours!" she replied.

"Yeah, but just once and . . ."

"Yeah, nice use of a condom. I probably have a baby and Messiah-groupie crabs."

I got down on my knees, and put my head to Romaya's stomach. I could feel her flinch slightly. It was too close. Too personal. But she did not stop me.

"You're pregnant," I said.

"For now." She was trying to find a tone that would

respectfully acknowledge all the miscarriages past without jinxing the present.

"I'll get a job," I said.

"That's not why I brought you the letter. I can take care of this baby. You need a job for you. I mean, what are you doing?"

"What am I doing?" I asked, getting back to my feet. "Haven't you heard? I'm leading a movement. I'm on the fucking news. Why do you have to make me feel like it's nothing?"

"Yeah, I know. I saw you on the news. Thanks for letting me know you were out of prison, by the way. They take away Facebook and you still find a way to make friends with thousands of people you don't actually know."

"They're not my friends. They're my followers," I said.

"Oh, sorry," she replied. "I should have said Twitter."

"You know what I mean."

"Yeah, I do. Instead of getting your own shit together, you're out saving the world."

"What do you care?" I asked. "I already tried to save you."

Now Romaya stood too. "I didn't ask you to be my savior."

"No, that's the point," I said. "You didn't even have to ask."

Tobey slammed on the brakes, and whatever staying power they build into Toyotas was burned to dust as we screeched toward a stopped bevy of Benzs, BMWs, and other cars I don't know.

"Jesus Christ," Jeeves shouted, grabbing the dash. We stopped short of the standstill, but there was clearly an accident ahead.

"Damn it," Tobey said. "Probably some asshole texting!"

"Really?" I asked. "See a lot of that in the Apocalypse, do ya?"

"Or looking in the mirror, I dunno," he said. He pulled out to the left and worked his way up until he could turn onto Beverly Drive. "Fuck this noise," he said. "We'll take Sunset Boulevard."

Romaya got up and went for the door.

"Please," I said. "Don't go."

She turned.

"Can't we try?" I asked. "We have a baby coming. We can do this. I love you."

Romaya looked at me like I was crazier than ever before.

"Where is this coming from?" she replied, taking two steps back, her hand almost on the door.

"What do you mean, where is it coming from? This isn't new," I said. "I've always loved you."

I took the love letter from my pocket. "Remember?" I asked. "I wrote it all down. Maybe you forgot because you gave it back to me."

I put it to her chest and she refused.

"No," she said. "It's too late, and . . . what the hell happened to it?"

The boy's blood was visible. "I was at that explosion at the Farmers Market. I helped a boy not bleed to death," I said.

"Really?"

"Yes, really. I do things. I'm doing something here, but that's not the point. I came here for you. Why else would I be in L.A.?"

"I dunno. Sounds like you came to lead a revolution?"

"No. I came for you."

"Then why aren't you with me?"

"Because you said no."

"Yeah, and that was enough?" she asked, and opened the door.

"What else am I supposed to do?" I asked, but she started to walk away. I shouted. "What else am I supposed to do?"

She stopped short, but came no closer. "I don't know, but Jesus, maybe if you weren't saving the world you'd think of something."

Tobey drove past the Beverly Hills Hotel and turned right on Sunset Boulevard. As the sun started to set, we reached the Sunset Strip. The lights and billboards reminded me a little of Times Square, but I didn't hear Gershwin the way I sometimes do when New York hits you just right. I heard eighties hair metal. *Paradise City* and just before it got worse and turned to Mötley Crüe, Tobey said, "Viper Room."

"Oh, shit, that's Book Soup," Jeeves said. "I've heard of that place. I've always wanted to go to a reading there."

"Yeah, and we passed the Hustler store," Tobey said. "I've always wanted to see if you could get a vintage pocket pussy shaped like Amber Lynn."

"Don't go," I said, and Romaya paused in my doorway. "We can do this. We can make it work."

Romaya looked at the floor. "She's not there," she said.

"Who?"

"Whoever it is you're looking for. She doesn't exist."

"What do you mean?" I asked, but she didn't answer. "Romaya, what are you talking about? You're right here, in my doorway."

"No one calls me Romaya but you," she said. "That's not even my name."

It was true. Romaya's name was Beth, but she hated it. Or at least she used to. She couldn't reconcile something so straightforward and all-American with the spice and fire that came with a last name like Petralia, and one day she simply crossed out Beth on her high school yearbook order form and wrote Romaya in its place. And just like that, she was Romaya. At least to me, when I met her in college. I liked the name, but I loved the audacity of the girl who renamed herself, and I never called her anything but that or Babe.

"Good-bye Romaya," I said, but she was already gone.

We passed the Comedy Store and Tobey told us he'd done a mic there, and about the mechanical bull at Saddle Ranch bar. Jeeves soaked it up, but I was losing more and more interest in this tour and even in where we were headed. All my thoughts were with Romaya.

"We should get a drink at Chateau Marmont while you're in town, Jeeves," Tobey said.

"Isn't that too swanky?"

"You'd think so, right?" he said. "And there *are* plenty of stars who live there months at a time, but it's still sorta weirdly undiscovered. Maybe people think they can't even try?"

We continued on as Sunset started to lose its glitz. Taco places, a Wendy's, a Ross Dress for Less. Oddly, it got worse and worse the closer we got to Hollywood.

"Check it out," Tobey said when we hit Highland. "Hollywood High School."

I looked at the school and its sign flanked by palm trees. I thought about the baby growing inside Romaya. I wondered how that child would know me if I weren't married to its mother. I wondered if it would grow up to go to school someplace where they shave trees to keep the rats away.

I didn't bother getting up from the floor when Romaya left Tobey's. It didn't seem possible. I was untethered— only in my body when angry and without the concentration even to maintain that anger. My thoughts fired intermittently through vapor.

That's the mess Jeeves found only minutes later. Tobey slept through Jeeves' knocking. When I didn't answer, he came in through the door Romaya had left ajar. He was wearing a Tool T-shirt; long, loose jean shorts; and flip-flops.

"You okay?" he asked, offering his hand, and I took it because refusing assistance would have required more words.

"Yeah, sure," I said. "Don't I look all right?"

"You've never looked worse."

"Oh. Well . . . you're not checking out my good side," I said, turning slightly.

He put his hands on my shoulders and then grabbed the sides of my face, hard. His fingers around the back of my head.

"Gladstone," he said. "How sad do you have to get before you stop making jokes?"

"I'm not sure, Dan. You gonna stick around to find out?"

"Do you want to talk about it?" he asked.

"Never."

Jeeves kept hold of my head and looked at me a little longer, making sure there was enough of me left behind my eyes, before saying, "Wake Tobey up. It's almost noon, and I have news."

Despite the directive, I promptly went to the fridge for a beer and sat down on the couch.

"Fine. I'll do it," he said, and in a few minutes returned with a very tired Tobey, who plopped himself down on the couch next to me.

Even Tobey could see the state I was in. "What's the matter with you?" he asked, but I just pointed to Jeeves standing over us, signifying the approaching lecture.

"That phone book you gave me to research?" Jeeves asked.

"Yeah?" Tobey replied.

"Well, that went kind of nowhere. I mean, I cut it down some. Checked the obits, found out who was dead, looked for connections, but that got me only so far. Even the people who are no longer with us, perhaps their secrets passed to another in a later iteration of the phone book. After a couple of days, I got pretty frustrated."

"Cool, so maybe I'm not an asshole," Tobey said. "Glad you got me up for that."

"Anyway," Jeeves said, "this morning I decided to take a break, and I thought I'd look into the history of the Hollywood sign, the way I'd mentioned."

"Oh my God," Tobey said. "Couldn't you just narrate this into your dream journal while I slept?"

"I'm getting there ADD boy. So those letters, they go way back. Started as part of some real-estate development, and they were never built with the intention of lasting."

"Isn't that everything in L.A.?" I asked.

"Until 1978, when a man gathered a group of investors to preserve the sign with corrugated steel. Know who that was?"

We didn't answer.

"It was Hugh Hefner," Jeeves said.

"Really?" I asked.

"Yep."

Tobey and I looked at each other. "That's interesting," I said.

"I didn't even get to the interesting part yet," Jeeves said, but then he took a breath and stopped. "Wait, why is that interesting?"

"Because we were at the Playboy Mansion yesterday," I said.

This time it was Jeeves who asked "Really?"

"Yes really. Special invitation."

I was about to tell him about Hamilton when Tobey interrupted.

"Yeah, I met that dude from *High School Musical*. He's a badass now. He did lines off Sasha Grey! Oh, FYI, she does porn that's not all about dudes blowing each other."

"Thanks for the heads up," Jeeves said, and looked at me disappointedly.

"Oh, I wasn't at that party, Dan," I said. "I spent my time talking to Hamilton Burke."

"You're joking. That's amazing."

"What kind of porn does he do?" Tobey asked.

"Shut up," I said. "You know who Hamilton Burke is from the journal. . . ."

"Not just from the journal," Jeeves said. "From, y'know, the world."

"All things being equal," Tobey said, "I'd rather be the dude doing lines off Sasha Grey."

"Please stop being yourself for a second," Jeeves urged. "We've hit upon more than we know. My point was that Hefner got eight donors besides himself to sponsor each letter with a contribution of twenty-nine thousand dollars. They were Terrence Donnelly, Giovanni Mazza, Les Kelley, Gene Autry, Andy Williams, Warner Brothers Records, Alice Cooper, and . . ."

We didn't guess.

"Hamilton Burke," Jeeves answered. "Hamilton Burke sponsored the 'D' in Hollywood."

"Well, yeah," I said. "I already knew Burke was a friend of Playboy, and he's got the cash. What's so surprising about that?"

"Because," Jeeves said. "Once I learned this little tidbit about the sign, just out of curiosity, I cross-referenced those nine names against the Internet phone book, and guess who was the only person there?"

"Hugh Hefner!" Tobey said.

"No, fuckwad," I said, turning to Tobey. "Hamilton Burke."

"Right," Jeeves said. "Burke, not Hefner, is in the phone book."

"Who cares?" Tobey asked.

"Who cares? What are you talking about?"

"Hear me out," Tobey said. "How much money did Hefner lose due to the Internet? I mean there are actual bona fide porno mags on the stands now. There are DVDs. Video killed the radio star, but the Internet killed magazine and videotape tits."

"Not familiar with that song," I said, "but it sounds catchy."

"It's not a bad theory, Tobey," Jeeves said. "But, y'know, you're ignoring the good evidence."

"You don't have shit," Tobey said. "You found an Internet phone book full of rich guys, and one of those rich guys did a rich-guy thing like sponsoring a Hollywood letter. Who gives a shit? Am I missing something?"

Now Jeeves sat down on the couch, weighted by his confusion. For the first time since I met him at Central Park, he was at a loss for words. Back then he was overcome with surprise and unable to express, calmly, that I was the Internet Messiah. But this time he was just confused like a normal person.

"I'm sorry," he said.

"What is it?" I asked.

"It doesn't happen often, but sometimes I don't separate my logical mind from my psychic one. . . ." He paused. "God, I hate to say this, but Tobey's right. I guess that's all I found, but in my gut, it *feels* like more. It *feels* significant."

"I don't want to gloat," Tobey said, "but are you admitting that the fact that a guy in the Internet phone book purchased the 'D' in the 'Hollywood' sign doesn't help us find the Internet?"

"Wait a second," I said. "That wasn't what Jeeves was researching. He was helping us narrow down the Internet phone book so we knew where to find the latest iteration. The version that has the fewest names, and therefore suspects. Or at least to find a way to narrow down the phone book we have."

"No, I know that," Jeeves said. "But does it really help us in any way? All we know is that Burke paid for a letter in the Hollywood hills."

And just like that, Jeeves, a man I'd met in Central Park months earlier, a man I was never supposed to meet again, brought another candle to my life. The bubbles sprang up and I screamed, "Son of a bitch!"

"What?" Tobey asked.

"Fucking Burke. He does know where the phone book is. And your feelings are right, Jeeves."

Tobey and Jeeves both moved closer, and even Tobey was open to the possibility of wonder.

"I know where the phone book is. The last thing Burke said to me? Happy hunting. There's gold in them thar hills."

"And?" Tobey asked.

"And let's get in the Matrix. Hamilton likes to fuck with me. The Hollywood sign. It's in the Hollywood Hills."

———

Highland became Cayuga and suddenly we were in a valley. But climbing. Jeeves looked out his window without any of the earnest cynicism or momentary confusion he exhibited in Tobey's apartment earlier. It felt good to see Jeeves open and naïve, and I wanted some of that, but I couldn't hold it. Not while I was treading life, weighted with so many new Romaya memories. I just tried to see the phone book in my mind. I thought about bringing it to her. Showing her my progress and accomplishment. Surely the man who could deliver this could find a way to create a happy life with her.

We kept going, following the road that overlooked the city until we made a right at Dark Canyon up top. And then we were there. The Oakwood Apartments. The rest of the journey would have to be on foot, but Oakwood's parking lot provided an excellent hiking access that would lead us all the way to the Hollywood sign, where I was sure Hamilton had buried the latest phone book. Under the "D."

11.

Minutes into our journey, we were all bleeding. Not that we were stupid. Tobey and I were wearing jeans, and while Jeeves was only in extra-long shorts, he did squeeze into a pair of Jynx's nearly knee-high black combat boots she'd left at Tobey's place. Still, those defenses weren't enough. The sticker bushes were merciless, especially when you were losing your footing on tiny gravel saboteurs. California provided natural ball bearings in the hundreds to ease you back into its finest fabric-piercing thorns.

After taking his third sticker bush to the knees, Jeeves asked, "You sure you know where you're going?"

"Yeah, I told you," Tobey said. "The month I moved out here from Michigan, I hiked this with some hippies.

"I thought you hated hippies," I said.

"I do, but who else would want to take mescaline with me under the Hollywood sign?"

We kept hiking up the back side of Cahuenga Peak getting farther and farther away from the somewhat convenient access point of the Oakwood Apartments parking lot we started from. We couldn't see our destination yet, but we did notice signs for Panasonic's "cutting edge security network."

"Huh, I never noticed those before," Tobey said.

"Really? Did you take the mescaline *before* the hike?"

"Maybe, or maybe I just didn't care then. I was getting high with hippies, not going on a covert mission as the co-Messiah of the Internet Reclamation Movement."

"Okay, two things," I said, literally pulling a sweating Jeeves up the hill behind me. "First, you're not the co-Messiah, you're the Tobey. And second, if you read the signs a little closer, you'll see they say the network of cameras is streamed for surveillance to recreation center headquarters via . . . *fiber optic cable*. So, yeah . . . oops."

That calmed Tobey for a while, but even after it left my lips, I knew that was no cause for comfort, as there was every chance a closed network could exist in the Apocalypse. Still, nothing was going to stop me now, so I was glad the techno-talk worked, and soon we were also distracted by the terrain. Things only got harder when we crossed the access road. I'm not sure at what point a hill becomes a mountain, but we started climbing side by side because single file would have meant taking a falling rock to the head. I didn't think Jeeves could make it, and I was thankful my three weeks in captivity had helped me shed those ten pounds that had bothered me for a decade. Jeeves was wheezing heavily, but the complaints were actually coming from Tobey.

"You better be right about this, Gladstone," he said. "I

was twenty-five the last time I tried this and yes, come to think of it, you're right. We were already tripping balls by this point. What sober person would do this?"

Sometimes you reach a point where the only thing that keeps you going forward is the fear of the road behind you. Sure, it was downhill, but that also probably meant falling. We'd have to face it at some point, but all I could tell myself now was that even though I was thirty-seven, there was no way I would fail to do something a high twenty-five-year-old Tobey had done. But that wasn't enough to propel me. And neither was the bullshit twinkle in Hamilton's eye, his goading clues or feigned interest in my existence. It wasn't even finding the clue that would bring us closer to knowing who had the power to steal the Net and, therefore, return it that kept me moving forward. It was the need to win. To claim a prize. A golden ticket. I wanted this phone book, and I wanted to hold it over my head like a boom box and prove to Romaya that my time away from her was not wasted. That I could get the job done. That I was strong enough to face anything.

I don't know what sustained Tobey and Jeeves. Maybe it was my newfound focus, but I do know it helped when we reached the top and saw water below. It looked darker than the surroundings, the sun having now set.

"Hey, that's the Hollywood Reservoir," Tobey said.

It doesn't seem possible that something man-made in the middle of Los Angeles could provide such comfort, but the climb leveled out and we could stand straight again. Sensing that freedom, we all sat down for real and rested. Tobey cracked open his backpack which, according to him, he hadn't opened since he first took this hill with the hippies.

"Anyone want some Faygo?" he asked, pulling out a half-decade-old soda bottle.

"Faygo?" I replied. "Were they hippies or Juggalos?"

"Shut up. I was broke when I moved here. Ralphs had a sale."

We sat for about twenty minutes, drinking Faygo (as well as the water Jeeves and I were smart enough to pack) while we watched our blood dry. There were eagles and condors overhead. All the masculine birds. And then we walked again until we could see the back of the Hollywood sign clearly below us. The letters were easily fifty feet tall, obscuring Los Angeles from directly below all the way to the ocean.

"It just occurred to me," Tobey said. "I mean, I think you're nuts, but *you* think we're at the hiding spot of the critical piece of evidence that will tell us which few people have the power to steal the Internet, right?"

"Right," I said.

"And you also think we don't have to worry about all the security cameras because there's no Internet, right?"

"Yeah."

"Well, I know I'm just some dumb shit who gets high all the time, but did it occur to you that maybe if you're right, the people who were powerful enough to steal the Net might want to protect their secrets?"

"Yeah, but you're forgetting one thing," I said. "I don't care. We're here. Somehow, we got to the clue that will break this open. And look! The sign's not even fenced in. They've just fenced the closest road to it. A road we never took because we're badasses. So I don't fucking care. I'm going."

Just then a black helicopter came into view, similar to those I first saw in Central Park, when New York shut down. Tobey, Jeeves, and I all hit the ground while its searchlight scanned the hills.

"Uh, you still going on?" Tobey asked.

"Yes! More than ever!" I shouted over the sound of propellers chopping the air. "The fact that there are black ops helicopters protecting this place proves I'm right."

"Well," Jeeves said. "Maybe it's just a normal helicopter, and maybe it's because the Net is down so the cameras aren't working, and they still want to police the area for trespassing and vandalism."

"Yeah, that," Tobey said.

I waited and watched the helicopter sweep over and get farther away. I was determined not to let it break our momentum. "Do you think I'm crazy, Jeeves?" I asked, but interrupted myself before he could reply. "I don't mean delusional crazy, in-need-of-help crazy. I mean, do you think it's crazy to believe there is a clue hiding up here?"

"Yes," he said. "It makes absolutely no logical sense that I can understand."

"Then why did you haul your ass up this mountain?" I asked.

"Because we're you're friends, asshole," Tobey said, and I could see even in the moonlight, they were both smiling. I supposed that should have been comforting—having two friends beside you to provide the strength to go somewhere you were afraid to go. But that's when I realized I hadn't taken a Wellbutrin in over a month and this was all too familiar. Once again, I'd gone to the heights of a coastal landmark in search of something improbable.

"Fuck!" I screamed, but neither Tobey nor Jeeves asked why. Maybe they thought I was angry about being thwarted by the helicopter, which now seemed to be looping around for a return sweep. Or maybe I'd been making friends again. The kind that don't exist or question you. I was scared, but I knew Wellbutrin wasn't an antipsychotic, and I was sober. And there was real blood making my jeans stick to my skin. There was dirt under my nails. But, ultimately, it was Jeeves who provided the most comfort.

"It's not just friendship," he said. "I do feel something. I don't know what I'm feeling, but you're right. This place is important. I just don't logically understand why. That's all I was saying. But that's always been the deal, right? From the very beginning, we knew you saw fantastic things. So either you're a crazy deluded mess or you are what I said you were over five months ago, in Central Park. So no, I don't understand why we are here or how this could be right, but I already went all in when I proclaimed a thirty-something drunk the Messiah."

"Well, then," I said, trying to sound like the more attractive of the two options, "let's get digging because we have a phone book to find, and I say it's right there."

I pointed to Hamilton's letter. The "D."

"Two problems," Jeeves said. "One, you're really not at all concerned about that helicopter? And two, did you bring a shovel?"

I was confident. "If they wanted me in jail, I'd be there already," I said. "They know I have nothing to do with these bombings, and surely that's a bigger concern than trespassing. And as far as the shovel, yeah . . ." I said, losing all momentum. "Fuck, yeah. No shovel."

"Not so fast, Mr. Pottymouth," Tobey said. "I think I have a hand spade in here at least. We used it to build a fire pit."

"How the fuck did you climb a mountain high on mescaline and then build a fire without killing yourself?"

"Well, one of the hippies did catch fire. We buried him somewhere around here with this," he said, pulling out the spade.

Jeeves and I looked around for a grave.

"Just kidding," Tobey said. "I mean, Starfinder totally did catch fire, but we put him out with the Faygo."

We worked our way down the mountain backwards, gripping at the grass and dirt to prevent ourselves from falling. The ground leveled out when we reached the back of the letters standing fifty feet tall in corrugated steel. We could still hear the helicopter, but not over us. A shovel would have been easier, but I was grateful for the spade. I was even grateful for Tobey despite all the shit he gave me while I dug sixteen, three-inch holes all around the "D."

Finally he said, "Look, if your D's turned up nothing may I again suggest digging under Hef's letter? I mean, he rebuilt this place. If he wanted to hide something, seems like that's the way to go. And I still think my porn theory for who stole the Net is better than your, y'know, no fucking theory."

I nodded at Tobey and then completely ignored him, holding the spade up to Jeeves. "Tell me where," I said.

"Boo," Tobey said. "Y'know, Jeeves is always looking for the D."

Jeeves and I turned to Tobey. "Was that just a joke about . . . man, you are the worst," I said.

"Actually, Gladstone," Jeeves said. "I was just about to make the same joke. Anyway, I'm out of touch with my feelings. I wish I could close my eyes and walk around this place without falling to my death. . . ." Jeeves took the spade and paced slowly behind the letters, holding onto them for support and making sure to avoid the pot-holes I'd made behind the "D." Then he kneeled behind the second "O" and ran his hand over the dirt, back and forth, before jabbing the spade into place. "Here," he said. "Best I got."

"Whose letter is that?" I asked.

"It's the one Alice Cooper bought."

Tobey was pleased. "Ooh, I like the sound of that."

I pulled back on the spade popping out a patch of dirt with the dig that Jeeves had already started. Then again and again as the helicopter grew louder and louder, re-turning from its loop and flying directly over us.

"We were totally just in its spotlight," Tobey shouted. "Maybe we should go."

"Leave if you want, Tobey," I said, shoveling as hard as I could. "I'm digging for gold."

Tobey worked his way a few feet down the front of the mountain, looking more nervous than I'd ever seen him, but he did not leave. Jeeves knelt down beside me and started using his hands to swipe away at the loose dirt until we could see more. Tobey contemplated the descent for the moment.

"What are you doing?" I asked.

"I'm plotting our escape in case we have to take off. We shouldn't go back the way we came. The hippies warned me. That access road we crossed is the first place they pick you up if you're spotted."

The theory made sense, but I didn't give it much thought. Probably because my next dig made a sound. A metal, prize-winning sound. I shoveled more. Each dig produced a thunk and a scrape.

"Hey, fuckwad," I shouted down to Tobey. "Why don't you come back and see how crazy I am now!"

Tobey joined us and I stopped digging so we could all stare at this shine in the Hollywood Hills together.

"Even the box is gold," I said. "Even the box!" I laughed and pulled the world's most needlessly ostentatious book holder out of the ground. Square, heavy, official, and with something definitely inside.

"It's locked," Tobey said.

"Well, y'know," I said, "I do know how to pick locks."

Jeeves put his arms around both of us.

"I'm sorry," Tobey said. "I'm proud of you, G-Sauce. You were right. I was wrong, and I'm sorry I doubted you. Repentant enough?"

It was the most sincere and forthright I'd ever seen Tobey and it felt very good to know he could be that way—pure—but our moment was interrupted when the helicopter returned. This time, however, it seemed to drop directly out of the sky, hanging in front of the letters.

We hid behind the "O" as a voice came from a bull-horn. "Halt!"

"Gladstone," Tobey said, "Jeeves and I will head for the access road. Wait 'til they follow us, and then bust down the front of the mountain."

"But the car's not there," I said.

"You'll end up in Burbank somewhere. You'll be fine. I mean, if you don't eat it falling down the front of the mountain. Just get that box opened and the book to Quiff."

"Good idea," Jeeves said to Tobey. "Man, you make it hard to hate you."

Using that compliment as jet fuel, Tobey busted back up the mountain as overtly as possible, with Jeeves tagging along behind. The helicopter rose higher in the sky and I put the box into my backpack so it wouldn't reflect the spotlight. I waited until Tobey and Jeeves got closer to the road and the helicopter followed, then I looked down the front of the hill. I stepped out from behind the "O" without being spotted, taking one last quick look through the hole before stepping forward. The second step didn't go as well and I lost my footing on gravel that sent my right leg shooting out while I slammed my left knee into the ground. There was no time to concentrate on the pain, though, because once I hit, especially with the weight of a backpack, I went into a roll. I couldn't see where I was falling, I didn't know when it would end and took comfort only in the density of the sticker bushes that snagged and slowed me as I tumbled. When I finally stopped moving, I looked up to find the sign more than fifty yards away, and seemingly on fire, but I assumed that was just the helicopter's searchlight flickering at the top of the mountain.

Over the next two or three hours I worked my way down, remaining fairly hidden in the dark and completely silent except when screaming from surprise sticker-bush attacks. But at least there were no more helicopters. And when the sun started to come up I could see the mountain had led out into some millionaire's backyard. I found a road and walked until I hit the town—Burbank I guess— and then I found an all-night diner that didn't mind serving some eggs and coffee to a man covered in dried blood and dirt.

My waitress gave me the name of a cab company and the diner even let me use their phone to make the call. Businesses were being nice about that now. Some people were asking them to reinstall pay phones. I thanked her and then noticed the cap of her pen had one of those metal clips you could break off.

"If I doubled your tip," I asked her, "do you think I could have your pen?"

"Are you serious?" she asked, looking down to make sure it didn't have some secret value.

"Yes, I need it."

"Go nuts," she said and dropped it with the check. I twisted off the metal clip and left a twenty for my ten-dollar meal.

"Thank you," she said.

"Not at all," I replied. "You wouldn't also happen to have a paper clip, would you?"

I gave the driver Romaya's address and worked my paper clip into a zigzag with two pennies between my fingers, and then I must have fallen asleep because he woke me in front of Romaya's, with my newly fashioned lock pick on the floor and drool running down my chin. According to my watch, it was 7:30 A.M., and I wondered if it was too early to ring her bell. But I didn't need to decide because Romaya actually rushed out of her door the second I left the cab. She was dressed like an adult again: blouse and skirt and everything.

"Babe," I called out, and she looked up in a panic. I was confused, but then I remembered what I looked like. I walked toward her as she stared.

"What happened to you?" she said. "Your coat is ruined."

"Hmm? Oh, yeah, Cali's been pretty hard on my sports jackets, I suppose. Don't worry," I said. "The letter's still fine." I pulled the love letter from my breast pocket just enough to prove it still existed, even if it was crusted with the boy's blood. "Where are you going, all dolled up?"

"Work," she said, dismissively.

"You got a job?" I asked.

"Just some stupid temp job for now."

"I told you I'd get a job," I said.

"Did you get one?" she asked.

"Well, no. It's been a day . . . but I have something else." I took off my backpack and removed the gold metal box.

"Baby or not, you need a job. You get that, right? You can't ignore that letter."

"I get it," I said, "but will you look?" I held up the box.

"What the hell is that?" she asked.

"The Internet phone book I told you about on the way to Google!" I said, but she didn't hear me because a helicopter was flying overhead.

"The Internet phone book!" I screamed. "The one I told you about! We found it!"

"What we?" she asked looking around.

"Tobey, Jeeves, and me."

"Jeeves is in California?" she asked.

"Yes."

"Where's Tobey?"

"With Jeeves. I think they might have gotten arrested. We got separated."

"Have you been taking your meds?" she asked.

"Dude, I'm showing you what I've done." I placed the box on the third step of the outdoor staircase leading up to the second-floor apartments. "I've found the biggest clue to who stole the Net—or at least, who had the power to."

Even Romaya had to be impressed. "It's locked," she said.

"Yes, but you know I can take care of that, right?" I took out the pen cap and paper clip.

"Oh, shit," she said.

I slid my pen cap tension wrench into place and raked my clip over the tumblers.

Romaya smiled. "I remember that sound."

"Me too. It feels just like the windows at Fordham."

I'd never picked a lock quicker than the night we snuck onto the law school roof, and I knew I couldn't beat it, but I was hoping to still make a strong showing. My first attempts did little more than dislodge dirt, and I readjusted my wrench.

"I really don't want to be late for my first day of work," Romaya said. "Even if it's a temp job. . . ."

"I got this," I said, and ran my pick with a touch more assertion and a drop less desperation. It popped. The locking mechanism actually dislodged and shot forward.

"Holy shit," Romaya said. "That's exactly like the Fordham windows!"

"Yeah, weird right? I've never seen that anywhere else."

"That was hot."

I opened the golden box and inside was a thin leatherbound book, much nicer than the earlier version Quiff had given me. The cover read. "Internet Control, Edition XXII."

"Now are you ready, Babe?" I asked, and I swear she was excited, even if she'd spent a decade scraping away at the possibility of wonder. I was putting her behind the scenes into a whole new world. "Here is the biggest clue of my investigation," I said, taking the book out for display. "The names of the people who have the ability to control the destiny of the Net. This is what Anonymous was looking for and couldn't find without me. I did this. Do you understand? Me. I found it."

She nodded in silence, and it will never be clear to me if her silence was born from suspense or good manners. I took out the book and there on the very first page of heavy parchment was the name I knew I'd see: Hamilton Burke.

"Look!" I said, handing her the book. "Look! Hamilton Burke. I've met him. Twice."

Romaya took the book from me. "The guy from your journal. The rich guy."

"Yes, I met him at the Playboy Mansion just the other day."

"You what?"

"Yes. I'm telling you, Babe. I'm not spinning my wheels here. I'm onto something."

"What were you doing at the Playboy Mansion?" she asked.

"Tobey and I got invited. By Hamilton!"

"So Tobey met Hamilton Burke too?" she asked, hoping to validate this story.

"Well, no. He went off with that douchebag from *High School Musical*, but I'm telling you. We had a drink and a cigar."

Romaya didn't say anything. She just flipped through the book. "There are some other names here too," she said as if choosing an appetizer from a menu she'd never seen before.

"Babe, I've won the trust of Anonymous and Jeeves. I've climbed the Hollywood Hills and found the clue no one else could find. Do you think anyone could do that?"

"No, but what's your point?"

"My point is marry me. If I can do this, can't I be the man you need?"

Romaya took a step back, unprepared. It wasn't just because we were divorced, but because she had been convinced for years before she left that I did not love her.

"Marry me," I said again, like it was a simple proposition. Like we had lived a life designed to deliver us to this conclusion as inevitably as the Hollywood Hills had delivered me to Burbank this morning. But again, she did not hear me over another helicopter. Without a wedding ring, I grabbed the gold box and held it up to her.

"You thought we got divorced because you couldn't crack conspiracies?"

"That's not the point."

"Then what's the point? This doesn't prove you love

me. If it proves anything, it proves you're the Internet Messiah."

"I don't want to be the Internet Messiah, I want you to love me again!"

"Aren't all those followers enough?"

"No. They're not. They're not nearly enough to replace everything. They don't fill the hole you left."

Those were still the wrong words, so I said what I almost said the day she left.

"Please. I'm still me. This is still my jacket. It's dirty and ruined, but it's still mine. It fits me. And it still has my love letter in its pocket."

She looked down at the gold box and back up at me. I felt she could see me a little more clearly now, but now that she was looking, she could also see the things I wasn't showing her.

"I know you're hurt," she said. "I'm hurt too, but isn't this the part where you're supposed to tell me you love me?"

I dropped down to one knee, saying, "I don't care about this. I care about you. I love you. Let's melt this fucker down to twenty wedding rings."

And then I heard a shot from behind me. I turned to find its location, but saw nothing aside from a helicopter flying away, and when I turned around, Romaya was on the ground, blood dripping from her mouth, breathing in spasms.

I held her head in my hands. "I'll get help!"

She grabbed both my lapels hard enough to keep me with her. She knew no ambulance would come in time. Instead, while she still could, she reached inside my jacket and pulled out the letter and held it to her chest as hard as she could before her head fell back to the ground.

"Babe!" I screamed into her face, but my voice bounced uselessly off the concrete around her. I held her until I felt my knees get wet. My bloody love letter clutched to her heart. Then I realized the blood was fresh. Wet. Her blood. And when I pulled it from her fingers I saw she'd grabbed the letter from the New York disability board. My love letter was still in my pocket. I sat there holding her. Everything in the darkness, wet with blood and tears, and at some point the life we created must have died inside her too.

12.

When I awoke, Romaya was gone, and I was in the back of Quiff's limo again. My clothes were still wet and filthy, but the Internet phone book was by my side. Quiff sat across from me in a Groucho Marx mask.

"I wish you'd called me sooner," he said, and then I remembered. After enough time had passed and I'd become as soaked as I could with Romaya, I'd managed to make my way into her apartment so I could call the number Quiff had given me days before. I let him know where I was, that I had the Internet phone book, and I asked him to come get me. Most of all, I insisted he bring an army.

Quiff could see me recovering the past. "You passed out from exhaustion nearly the moment we came," he said. "You've been through a lot. And without much sleep it seems." He paused and then added, "I'm sorry about Romaya."

"Where is she?" I looked out the window and saw we were no longer in Brentwood.

"We called the shooting into the police. I'm sure they have . . . her now. Again, I'm sorry."

It only took a moment of being awake to regather my focus and anger. "It was him," I said. "It was Hamilton Burke. We have to kill him."

"Hold on," Quiff said. "How do you know it was Burke?"

"He's here. In the book!"

I tossed the Internet phone book onto Quiff's lap and he started flipping the pages.

"Y'know, Gladstone," he said, "there's more than just one name in here. Did you even bother to read past the first page?"

"I didn't need to, did I? It's him. He tried to kill me, but when I dropped to one knee to propose to Romaya, he shot her by mistake. Or one of his assassins did, I mean. Listen to me. I don't care about the Net. I just want him dead."

"This is the same Gladstone who wasn't looking for war? The Gladstone who believed in 'pure things'?"

"Well, things have changed," I said. "He killed Romaya. I want him dead."

"You want one of the most successful, powerful, and richest men in the world dead?"

"Yes!"

"Well, I'm not sure I can help you there, Gladstone."

"Why? You want to bring him down from the inside? Do all your Anonymous computer-hacking bullshit? Without the Internet? You said you had an army!"

"I do have an army, Gladstone. You have no idea. But I just can't go ahead with your plan."

"Why not?"

Quiff dropped his head down almost to his knees, until I could see the seam at the back of his mask. He grasped the rubber at the top and pulled it forward off his face before looking up at me with a smile.

"It's nice to see you again, Wayne," he said.

It was Hamilton Burke. The same man from New York. The same man from the Playboy Mansion. It was Hamilton Burke. Sitting with me. Talking with me.

"What have you done to Quiff?" I asked, and he frowned with impossible disappointment until I understood.

"There is no Quiff?" I asked. "It's always been you?"

"Right."

"In New York, in California, always?"

"Correct." He paused and leaned in a little closer, speaking in a needless half whisper. "I like to know what's going on," he said. "Anonymous? If there's gonna be an antiestablishment, well then you know the establishment better be part of it. You can never have too much information."

He paused for emphasis. "I've always found, well, people who only know part of the story make poor choices. Don't you agree?"

Hamilton had seen me drunk and crazy. He'd seen me sober and insecure. But he had no way to predict what I'd do next. I launched forward in my seat and grabbed tight and quick at his throat, banging his head up against the glass that divided us from the front. Before I could bash his head a second time, the glass lowered and one of his masked goons leaned forward over Hamilton's shoulder, sticking the barrel of a gun in my face. He didn't wait for me to release Hamilton. He just jabbed the side of the revolver into my forehead, sending me backwards and bloody into my seat.

"Come now, Wayne. Did you think I would leave myself exposed the moment after telling you who I was?" Hamilton asked. "I'm fucking Hamilton Burke. I didn't inherit this position from my dad, y'know?"

"Fuck you," I said, holding my head.

"Look, you're upset. That's understandable. Tell you what: I'm going to raise this glass again so we can talk without these ruffians. But make no mistake, they can see through their side and their guns are pointed at you."

Hamilton looked at me while I tried to remember everything I had confided in him when I thought he was a friend. Then he poured himself a drink from the decanter he didn't let me touch the last time I was in this car.

"Beauté de Siècle by Hennessy," he said. "Y'know, you *really* pissed me off when you drank my Scotch that first time. And smoked my Cuban in New York for that matter. For someone who'll never earn north of $150,000 a year, you sure do have expensive tastes."

"Why is it," I asked, "that the rich are the cheapest fucks alive?"

Another frown. "Is that what you really want to ask me, Mr. Gladstone? Why don't you ask me your real question?"

He was right, and I needed to know, but I was consumed by that feeling of inferiority Hamilton was so good at infusing. "Before I ask," I said, "will one of your goons shoot me if I pour myself a drink of your expensive Scotch?"

"Forget about the goons," Hamilton said. "I won't let you."

"That's okay," I said. "I didn't really want it."

"No?" he asked, leaning forward and swirling his drink in its glass.

"No," I said, and slapped the drink out of his hand, spilling it onto the floor of his car.

"Well, you certainly showed me," he said, pouring himself a new drink as easily as pulling a second tissue from a box of Kleenex.

"My question, Hamilton, is . . . why me?"

He laughed, spritzing the remnants of his drink from his old man's lips.

"Oh, I'm sorry," he said, wiping his mouth, "but that's not the question I was expecting. That's the problem with your generation. Everything's always about you! It's not. You're not the important one. I am." He took a sip of his drink. "I am the establishment. I am the antiestablishment. You think you're the only would-be Messiah I kept tabs on? You think you're the only fucking nothing who wants to be a hero? The world is filled with people like you. You're not the first, second, or last man I constructed stories for and spun in circles.

"Hell, when the government locked you up and it seemed your buddy Tobey might be my next concern, I took an interest in him too. I'm very interested in anything that can be in my way."

Hamilton paused to catch his breath, and in that moment he almost seemed to feel bad for me.

"Aww, don't look at me like that," he said. "Don't you know I like you? You rose above the other nothings. You started a movement. That's why I couldn't just kill you. You're no good to me as a martyr. You have talents. So many that I really don't understand how you've wasted your life so."

"Thanks Hamilton," I said. "I'll tell everyone you thought so when I'm pissing on your grave."

"That's no way to talk," he said. "Do you know how much work I put into you? I didn't have to go that extra mile. I read your book, I gave you a mission. I commissioned a chopper to bury some treasure for you. That box wasn't cheap. And how about that lock? Do you know I had a guy fashion a lock for you exactly like the ones you described in your book, on your Fordham law school windows? Just so you could be a hero. Did that make you feel good? And even the letter I planted it under. I thought you'd like that."

"I'm not a big Alice Cooper fan," I said.

"No, not Cooper. He paid the cash, but he bought the letter in Groucho's name." Hamilton held up the mask. "Y'know, because your whole mission's a joke!"

I had to hold back tears, not so much because of everything that had happened, but because I had tied my life to someone who wanted me to cry.

"What?" he said. "I thought you liked jokes, Gladstone."

Hamilton could somehow embody both intense disdain and impersonal indifference without a trace of shame. Only my years on comment threads could have prepared me for such a thing.

"Look on the bright side, Gladstone," he said. "I taught you some things."

"Yeah, stuff like how in these times you can only trust a man in a mask."

Hamilton paused and lit a Cuban. "Ah, that. Yeah, well, sorry. Y'see, in some ways that's true. I mean, with communication, and cookies, and data mining you really can't be too careful. . . . But here's the thing about a man in mask," he said, exhaling, "and I'm really disappointed you didn't realize this, but the reason you can't actually trust a man in a mask is . . . he's still wearing a fucking mask!"

"Sorry I disappointed you, sir."

"The only people you can trust are those too weak to hurt you," he said.

"Does that mean you trust me?" I asked, but he didn't answer.

"Y'know, you might not believe this," he said, "but I first took down the Net to help men like you. That stuff I told you in New York is true. It's a rigged game, our system, and I'd won it. Thought it might be nice to go the other way with my remaining years."

I was getting cold. My shirt was so wet with blood I started to shiver from the AC. I tried to open the window, but it was locked.

"Why don't you just kill me," I said. "I'm not interested in getting to know you."

He continued. "I took down the Net at the hubs," he said. "You didn't even ask."

"I'm sorry," I said. "Did you like taking the Net down at the hubs? Did that finally give you an erection?"

You can't hurt a man like Hamilton with facts, and anger is just a sign of weakness.

"I mean, I owned interests in enough companies to gain access," he said, ignoring me. "And when you have far too much money to spend in ten lifetimes, it's easy to bribe people to make things not work. Certain interruptions. I was just playing at first. Disrupting signals at certain points. Rewriting code to send users to the wrong Web sites."

"Some people get a dog. Take up fishing."

"I just wanted to see if I could do it. And don't pretend you don't remember why. You practically memorized every word I said for your little book. The Net screws the working man. It increases a worker's productivity. But more importantly, it increases the employer's expectation of productivity. You're never free. You are always on."

"Maybe you just missed sexually harassing the secretary who used to take your dictation."

"I'm glad your penis still works, Gladstone, but is that all you want to talk about? I was saying, ultimately, I needed more and more collaborators to keep the world offline. And that was okay, too. I was always good at consensus building, but that's not important. What's important was the moment I saw I could take it down, I saw an angle. I didn't invent the most important technology of the twenty-first century, but if I could be the one to bring it back—well then, that's almost as good. People would pay for that. People will pay for that. And we can do away with this well-meaning, virtually free, wasted venture, I'll bring it back on my terms. So y'see, you're not even needed, Mr. Gladstone. The Net will return with or without you. When the people are ready to receive it in a different way. This Apocalypse is merely a palate cleanser."

I looked out the window and saw signs for LAX.

"Why are we going to the airport, Hamilton?"

"Because," he said. "This morning you went to the bank and withdrew the last $3,000 to your name."

"Why would I do that?"

He reached into his robe and pulled out a wad of hundreds and threw them in my lap. "Because you needed the money," he said. "I'm guessing you thought you'd be leaving the country."

"I don't have a passport."

"Don't you?" he asked, and threw one on my lap to go with with cash. "Smart guy like you would want to take care of everything before murdering his estranged wife."

Now the affability was gone. Hamilton was no longer privately amused by his cutting, witty banter. He was showing me who he was. He was revealing the full absence of rules or conscience that would prevent lesser men from visiting full evil upon their enemies.

"You went to see your wife, Gladstone. She's dead now. You left the scene without even calling the police. Your two best friends in the world, Tobey and Jeeves? They're in custody. And do you know what the government will find when they investigate those bombings further? They'll trace them back to the Internet Reclamation Movement."

"Tobey wouldn't do that."

"Tobey doesn't sweat the details like you, and he has no idea what was done on his watch. Besides, I'm not just talking about the Farmers Market. Personally, I think the government has a much better case against your friends for the Hollywood sign."

"Trespassing."

"No, they blew up the 'D' last night after scrawling Messiah graffiti all over the other letters. You probably haven't heard the news yet."

I remembered the fire I'd seen after my fall down the mountain.

"Face it: You have blood on your hands, Mr. Gladstone. Literally. Look at you. Is this what good men look like? Are they covered in the blood of their dead wife?

Are their best friends held as persons of interest by the government? Do they have absolutely no income—not even the disability they sucked down like a parasite for years? Are they all alone on the wrong side of their country? This is what you get believing in pure things. Nothing. Because nothing is pure. Not even you, Mr. Gladstone, and it's time for you to go."

The car pulled over to the taxi stand and Hamilton threw open the door.

"Any last words?" Hamilton asked.

I couldn't speak. I was afraid if I opened my mouth I'd vomit, even though my throat felt as clamped as my stomach. How could I really be sitting with the most powerful man in the world, and how could he really have conspired to destroy me?

"Is this really happening?" I asked.

"So many questions, Mr. Gladstone, but not the right one. Yes, this is really happening," he answered.

"It's not just another delusion?"

"What do you mean?" he asked, cautiously optimistic.

"I haven't gone to therapy. I haven't taken my pills. I haven't been sleeping. . . ."

"What are you asking me, Mr. Gladstone?" He was almost there.

"Is everything all right? Is Romaya alive? Is the world still the world?"

"How could that be?" he asked. "What are you asking?"

I stared into his blue eyes. No mask. Nothing blocking me from who he was. "Tell me I'm just crazy," I begged.

Only then did Hamilton release his full smile. "Sorry, Mr. Gladstone," he said. "Not this time."

Epilogue

EXCERPT FROM THE REPORTS OF
FORMER SPECIAL AGENT
AARON N. ROWSDOWER
LOS ANGELES, CALIFORNIA

Life has no shortage of rough edges and cruel angles. It's virtually impossible to navigate the twists and turns without getting cut eventually. Usually, these minor insults and traumas heal. Sometimes they don't. Not fully anyway. And if you accumulate enough scar tissue, you can stop working the way you're supposed to. You break.

They say what doesn't kill you makes you stronger, and I guess for some, that's true. After all, pain makes you flinch. Your fingers form a fist, and that fist can become

tighter and harder with each indignity suffered. Eventually, that fist might even get
strong enough to punch down walls. But if
you need your hand for something other than
violence, if you want to unfurl those fingers
to caress a loved one or comfort someone in
need, and can't, well then, you're broken.

I met so many men like that when I was an
agent, and you can learn a lot from what
breaks a man in the same way studying a gun-
shot wound can tell you all about the weapon
and how it was fired. For example, they may
say a woman was shot to death at close range
by an angry ex-husband, but any examiner
worth his salt will write a report that shows
it was a rifle shot from a distance. You can
study the bullet's trajectory, seeing how it
tore through the left ventricle and exited
the spine by T12 to determine it was fired
from a high angle. You can divine all of that
from examining the victim. And even if that
report is lost and the body is then cre-
mated, it doesn't change the truth.

It has been two months, one week, and six
days since anyone has last seen him. Almost
the same amount of time the United States
government has no longer needed my services. I could complain more, but I'll save
that for a blog for when the Net comes back.
I suppose I could look for a new job. A new
career. Security. Consulting. Hell, maybe
I'll even put that J.D. to use and take the

bar. But these days it seems to me the only
thing I should be looking for is Gladstone,
the unknown man who ended up with too many
names. Internet Messiah, The Meme-Siah, mur-
derer, terrorist. But I'll go with just Gladstone because nothing's quite sticking yet
to this inkblot man.

And maybe that's how he wanted it. It
seemed so in his final address at The Hash
Tag. I was there, and although he didn't
know, I took a handful of those paper do-it-
yourself memes featuring blank lines and a
WiFi symbol wearing an M-shaped fedora. And
now they're everywhere. Left behind in coffee shops and train stations. Spray-painted
on walls. No one in the real world is calling
for the Messiah's freedom or prosecution. Instead, they're talking about the Internet as
simply as they can. Spreading the message
without the help of fiber optic cable. There
are sweet memes like "The Internet is . . .
an e-mail from my boyfriend overseas." There
are practical ones like "The Internet is . . .
seeing my children on camera while I'm away."
And then, of course, there are the political
ones like "The Internet is . . . sharing information regarding our oppression."

But the best one I saw had been spray
painted in black on the wall outside
the L.A. Veterans Affairs building where
we'd been holding Gladstone. It popped up
the day I was told my services were no lon-

ger needed, and seeing it helped just a little because as I walked away, the building's tall white walls now read in fifteen-foot letters:

The Internet is . . .

People. And We're Still Here.

I'm going to find Gladstone and tell him about that. I hope it brings some comfort, but I'm not looking to heal him. I need his cuts and bruises. I need to examine the body. Before I was terminated, I got a chance to speak with Tobey, who was being held as a person of interest and domestic-terror suspect. I asked him if he thought I'd find Gladstone alive. He wasn't feeling talkative, still in that stage of capture where you resent your coconspirators even when insisting there's no conspiracy. He did say, however, that dying wasn't an option for Gladstone, because then he'd have to stop whining.

I'm counting on that, on his capacity for pain. Because each blow I study will tell me something more about what we're up against. I know Gladstone saw his wife die in front of him, but he saw something even more than that to send him running. Worse than running—hiding. This is no subway escape to a drunken weekend. He's seen something dark enough to keep him hidden. And I want to see the burns so I recognize that branding iron and the men who carry it when they come for me.

Maybe we'll find the Net, but first I'm going to do what I do. I'm going to find my man. I've already done what any investigator would do: checked the airports, the bank accounts and transactions. I found the withdrawn money and the plane ticket purchased in cash. And then I did something else, on a whim. I checked the airport's lost and found. Several. There's not just one. And do you know what I found? His grandfather's fedora, thrashed and bloodstained. I had it cleaned up for him. They did what they could. It helped a bit. It will be nice to bring him something other than my microscope for his pain. And in the meantime, I'm wearing it. I hope it brings me luck.

According to the label, the hat is from New York, and so am I. As I sit here and look out my window, I think about how we'd both like to go home, and someday I hope we will. Gladstone too. But there's still work to do and New York is not where this plane is headed.

Acknowledgments

This novel exists because my editor, Peter Joseph, had faith in it before it was even written. And it exists in its current form because he allowed me the time and freedom to keep working until it was the book I wanted it to be. Of course my agent, Lauren Abramo, also ensured its creation by believing in Book One of this trilogy, and getting it published in the first place before continuing on as my personal sherpa through the labyrinth of publishing and neurosis.

Thank you to everyone who was good enough to buy *Notes from the Internet Apocalypse*. That tangible level of interest was tremendously encouraging as I worked to deliver this novel. And while we're discussing Book One, thank you to Liz Coleman for supporting that project so fiercely and teaching me how speak Australian.

This book was also made possible by Carl, Amy Jo, Ruari, Evi, and everyone at The Growler who kept me in

Jamesons and fried pickles during its final stages. Thank you also to all the early readers of this book for their time and input. It is greatly appreciated. And thank you to Randall Maynard for all the art and kindness he has given me.

Lastly, I need to thank Maura Chwastyk. Unlike Book One, *Agents of the Internet Apocalypse* is an L.A. story. While I have been to Los Angeles on several occasions, and the story is meant to be told from the perspective of a visitor, countless times during the writing of this book, I still needed inside information. Something beyond a traveler's impressions or the details of an Internet search. I needed someone to help me see. Someone not only to hold up an L.A. scene, but to focus on the same details I would, if my eyes were fixed on that setting. I was very lucky to meet Maura, a Los Angeles expatriate, during the writing of this book. She was an invaluable resource, delivering such carefully observed details that it became my job as writer not to destroy the inherent magic of her impressions as I pulled them from her e-mails and fastened them to the page.